ACCUSED

"She was with them," he was saying. "The money's in her knapsack. She's one of the robbers!"

I went numb with shock. I thought I was losing my mind.

"I don't understand," I said. "The guy with the gun—you saw him force me to go with him. The short guy's got the money. . . . You've got to know I'm innocent! I can't be arrested, can I?"

"Danielle Nelli?" he asked, as if he had never heard the name before. "You have the right to remain silent. You have the right to counsel. Anything you say may be used against you . . ."

Other Avon Flare Books by
Elizabeth Levy

DOUBLE STANDARD

THE DANI TRAP

ELIZABETH LEVY

AN AVON  FLARE BOOK

AVON BOOKS
A division of
The Hearst Corporation
1790 Broadway
New York, New York 10019

The William Morrow edition contains the following Library of
Congress Cataloging in Publication Data:

  Levy, Elizabeth. The Dani trap.
  Summary: Shortly after sixteen-year-old Dani volunteers to work undercover
in a police investigation of illegal liquor sales to teenagers, she finds herself
being framed as an accomplice in a liquor-store holdup.
  [1. Mystery and detective stories. 2. Police—Fiction. 3. Alcohol—
Fiction] I. Title.
PZ7.L5827Dan 1984   [Fic.] 84-9025

First Flare Printing, April 1986

FLARE TRADEMARK REG. U. S. PAT. OFF. AND IN
OTHER COUNTRIES, MARCA REGISTRADA, HECHO EN
U.S.A.

Printed in the U.S.A.

K-R 10 9 8 7 6 5 4 3 2 1

To Mara,
who knows how to get us out of traps

ONE

I was not drunk. But Michael was. He controlled the automatic windows from the driver's side, and he was having a wonderful time making them go up and down. The cool April air made me shiver.

"Come a little closer, Dani," Michael said. "I'll keep you warm."

I inched across the seat as far as the seat belt would let me. The way Michael was driving, I wasn't going to take off that seat belt for anything. Michael put his arm around me, but I was still shivering. I looked out at the reflectors on the shoulders of the highway. They were whizzing by too fast to count.

Michael squeezed my shoulder. "Don't be so uptight. I'm not really drunk—not half as drunk as your friend back there at the party."

He was talking about Raynor. Raynor had tried to stop me from going for a drive with Michael because Michael was drunk. The only trouble was that Raynor was even drunker.

Until the seniors had crashed Bonnie's party, none of us had been drinking. But the next thing I knew, some bottles from Bonnie's parents' liquor cabinet were out on the counter, and Bonnie had a stricken look on her face.

"So is Raynor your boyfriend?" asked Michael. He gave my shoulder another squeeze.

"No, he's one of my best friends." He and Bonnie have been my best friends since seventh grade.

"Best friends?" Michael looked at me quizzically as if he didn't believe me.

"What's wrong with that?" I asked.

"I know it's cool to have girls as friends, but I've never been just friends with a girl. I guess I'm just a man's man."

I wanted to laugh out loud. It was such a silly, macho thing to say. Raynor would be doubled over laughing if he could have heard. "What's a 'man's man,' Michael?" I asked. I ran my hand through my new punk haircut. My hair was shorter than Michael's.

Michael laughed. "Sorry. I guess that was a stupid thing to say."

"Yeah, it was," I agreed.

"You don't let a guy off easy. I like your spirit."

If I really had spirit I'd have had the nerve to tell Michael he was driving too fast. I was in an advanced history class with him, but until the party, he had never paid much attention to me.

Michael took his arm from around my shoulder and reached into his parka pocket. He pulled out a plastic water bottle.

"Want a sip? It's tequila and o.j."

I shook my head. "No, I—"

I never finished the sentence. I never saw the animal dart out. I only heard the thud, and then the car swerved out of control, across the shoulder of the highway and into a ditch. My seat belt probably saved my life, but even with it my body was whipped back and forth on my seat. Whiplash is not just a word. I felt like a whip lashing back and forth.

2

The car rocked. It felt as if we were going to roll over. I heard Michael yelling. Then slowly the car stopped rocking, and we were still right side up.

Michael was slamming his fist against the steering wheel. I wasn't sure, but I thought he was crying.

"Michael?" I whispered. "Are you okay?"

"I'm okay," he snarled. "Dumb animal."

I waited for him to ask me if I was all right, but instead he opened the car door and went out to inspect the damage. I got out, but it wasn't easy. My legs were trembling uncontrollably.

Finally Michael turned to me. "You okay?" he asked over the top of the car.

"I think so," I said, trying to keep my voice from shaking. I looked down the highway. No other cars were in sight. "But didn't we hit something? I heard a thud."

"Get back in the car," ordered Michael. "Everything looks okay. Maybe it'll start."

I ignored him and climbed up the embankment. Lying on the highway I saw what looked like a laundry bag that had fallen off the back of a truck. Then I heard a whimper. I ran out into the middle of the highway. It was a large dog. Its rib cage was heaving. I could hear it struggling to breathe.

The dog snarled as I came close. "It's okay, boy," I whispered, knowing I was lying. The dog laid its head back down on the highway.

"Michael!" I called. "Come here. It's a dog, and he's hurt. We've got to get him to a vet."

"Get out of the middle of the highway," Michael shouted. "Do you want to get yourself killed?"

"He's alive. You've got to help me."

I had to get the dog to the side of the road. If a car came tearing around the cuve, we would both be killed. I waited for Michael to help me. Then I heard a retching noise. Michael was kneeling and vomiting.

I put my arms under the dog's belly. "It's you and me, baby," I whispered to the dog. "I just hope I don't hurt you."

Seconds later a car streaked by without stopping. I felt the blast of cold air as it went by.

I saw the headlights of Michael's car go on down in the embankment. "I've got to get out of here," he shouted. "Don't you realize how much trouble I could get in? I could get my license taken away."

Michael revved his engine. "We can't go without this dog," I shouted back. "We can't just abandon him. I'm not going. I'm not leaving this dog here to die."

Michael got out of the car again. He slammed the door and strode over. He looked like he wanted to kick me and the dog. But he knelt beside me.

"Is he really still alive?" Michael asked.

I nodded. "We could take him to the animal clinic behind my house. Dr. Vickers lives there. She'll help me. We take our cats there all the time."

Michael wasn't listening to me. I followed his eyes down the highway. I could just see the flashing red light of a police car.

Michael swore under his breath. He grabbed my arm. "Forget about the dog. The police will help him. I think he's going to die anyway."

I was pretty sure that Michael was right. But I couldn't just leave the dog. "You go," I said.

"Look, they might bring me in for drunk driving. I don't think I can pass the stupid breath test. They'll put me away. New Jersey laws are really rough."

"Get going, then," I said. "The police'll take me to the vet."

Michael gave me a last look. "What a night," he muttered. "Thanks. I owe you one."

He got back in his car. I felt relieved when the engine turned over. I didn't want him to get into trouble. I could see the police car coming closer. My blood was racing as if the police were coming to arrest me, though I knew I hadn't done anything wrong. At least, not technically wrong.

Michael's car made it over the embankment and back out onto the highway. He took off, fast. I waved my arms above my head so the police car would see me and the dog. I was almost blinded by the headlights.

The police car pulled over to the side, about fifty feet away. A police officer ran over to me. He was young, with wavy brown hair. The headlights from the police car made the curls on his head look like angel fluff. Don't ask me how come I noticed something like that, but later, when I told that detail to Raynor and Bonnie, they both laughed at me.

"Are you all right?" the police officer asked.

To my surprise I burst into tears. He sounded so much more concerned about me than Michael had been, and he didn't even know me.

I nodded, wiping away my tears with the back of my hand. I didn't want him to think I was a baby. "I'm fine, but this dog is hurt."

The police officer knelt beside me. "Is he yours?" he asked.

I shook my head no. Suddenly I realized my predicament. It wasn't going to be easy to explain what I was doing in the middle of the highway at eleven o'clock at night.

"I . . . I found him. . . ."

"Found him?" Another police officer was now

5

standing over me. "You just happened to be wandering around the highway?" She didn't believe me, and I couldn't blame her.

"Please, just help me get the dog to the vet's. There's a clinic right behind my house."

"Who was in that car we saw take off?" she asked.

"Please," I pleaded. "This dog is dying."

"She's drunk," said the woman police officer. "I can smell it from here. Stand up. Let's see you walk a straight line. I'll go get the breathalyser. You have the right to refuse the test. But then we have the right to take you in."

I realized that I did smell of alcohol. Michael's tequilla and o.j. must have spilled all over me when we had the accident.

"How can you arrest me for drunk driving?" I asked, thinking fast. "I don't even have a car." The police officer gave me a look like she thought I was being a wisemouth. I was just telling the truth.

"Come on," said the wavy-haired officer. "She's just a kid. Let's take her home and get the dog to a vet. Then we can ask questions." He lifted the dog easily and put him in the backseat of the police car. "Get in here with him," he said to me. "By the way, what's your name?"

"Danielle Nelli." I saw the police officer write it down in her notebook. She got behind the wheel. "Where do you live?" she asked.

I gave her my address.

"I know where it is," she said.

The backseat of the police car was separated from the front by steel mesh. I looked at the backs of the two police officers through the mesh, and I knew why Michael had been terrified. He would never have been able to walk a straight line. I was frightened. I had been so worried about the dog that I hadn't realized that the police might not believe me. Now I was in the backseat of a police car with a dying dog. And in just a few minutes, I was going to have to face my parents.

TWO

The tires of the police car squealed as we turned into our driveway. I uttered a little prayer of thanks that we had arrived in one piece. The police officer drove as if she didn't have to worry about any speed limit, and I guess she didn't. She was the law.

The police officers flanked me on both sides as we walked up the steps of our front porch, like I was a prisoner they wanted to make sure wouldn't escape. The lights in our living room were still on. I knew my parents were up. I could hear the television set through the open window.

Mom came to the door. She was barefoot and dressed in an old jumpsuit with baggy knees.

When she saw me with the two police officers, she put her hand to her mouth and stifled a scream. Then she opened her arms and drew me to her. "Dani . . . did you have an accident?"

My father was at the door in seconds.

Mom looked up at the police officers. "What happened?" she asked.

"We found her out on the highway, ma'am."

"What!" exclaimed my father.

"I found a dog that was hit by a car," I said quickly. I didn't have the nerve to tell my parents I was in the car that hit the dog. "We've got to get him over to Dr. Vickers. He's in the back of the police car.''

My father looked at the police officers. "A dog?"

"Yes, sir," said the woman officer. "It looks likes it's in bad shape.''

"I'll go call Dr. Vickers," said my mother, immediately moving into action.

My father helped get the dog out of the car. We all went over to Dr. Vickers's clinic.

I was left alone on the lawn with my mother as the police officers took the dog inside. She must have sensed how alone I felt. She put her arm around my shoulder. "Dr. Vickers will do all she can," she said.

My father and the police officers came back out seconds later. "She says he's in pretty bad shape," said my father.

"We'd like to ask your daughter some questions," said the woman police officer.

"So would we," said my father.

"Why don't we all go into the house," said my mother. As we walked back, I had trouble keeping myself from shaking.

I felt like sobbing, but I wasn't going to cry in front of the police.

"I'll make you a cup of tea," my father said to me. "Officers, would you like tea or coffee?"

"Nothing, thanks," said the policeman. "Don't I know you? You're Ed Nelli, the legal aid lawyer. I thought the name Nelli sounded familiar. I'm John Nelson. This is Officer Martin.''

Officer Martin extended her hand. "I've run into you, too. You once gave me a hard time on cross-examination. You got your client off, didn't you?"

"I recognize you both," said my father, shaking

their hands. My father worked as a lawyer for the state, representing clients who couldn't afford to pay a private lawyer's fees. That meant that Dad made far less money than most lawyers.

My father handed me a cup of tea with honey in it. "This will warm you up," he said. "All right, tell me what happened."

"Well, we found her alone on the highway—" said Officer Nelson.

My father interrupted. "Excuse me," he said. "I'd rather Dani tell me herself."

I stared into my tea cup as if it were possible to read the future from a tea bag.

"What happened, Dani?" asked my mother.

"I didn't do anything wrong," I said.

"Nobody's accusing you of anything," said my father. "But you were supposed to be at a party at Bonnie's, and you come home with two police officers and a wounded dog. We have a right to know what's going on."

"I went for a ride with a friend," I said.

"Who?" asked Officer Martin.

My father ignored the officer's question. "Just tell us the rest in your own words," he said.

"We just went out for some air, Dad. It got stuffy in Bonnie's basement. We took a ride, and we found the dog. I stayed with him, but my friend had to leave." I muttered the last words into my tea cup. I knew my story didn't make sense. I just prayed that my parents wouldn't make me give Michael's name to the police.

"Had to leave?" snorted Officer Nelson. "We saw a car pull away as we came toward her."

"I didn't do *anything* wrong," I repeated. "He didn't do anything wrong, either. You're acting like we both did something against the law. All I did was try to save the poor dog. Is that a crime?" I was sobbing.

"Take it easy, honey," said my father.

My mother stood up. "Thank you, officers," she said. "I think we can handle this now."

The two police officers looked surprised. "Aren't you going to make her give us the name of the guy she was with?" asked Officer Martin almost angrily.

My mother shook her head. "I think that's for us to discuss with Dani alone, don't you, Ed?"

My father nodded, but he seemed lost in thought.

Mom showed them to the door. They still looked as if they wanted to stay and cross-examine me, but my mother had made up her mind and nothing could change it. Not even police officers.

"I think you should know, Mrs. Nelli, that Dani smelled of liquor."

"Dani doesn't drink," my mother said.

"All parents think that," said Officer Martin.

"Did she act drunk?" my mother asked.

"No," she admitted.

My father said, "I don't think there is a law against asking police officers to help with an injured dog, even if you are drunk."

"If you're under twenty-one in this state, it's against the law to *be* drunk," countered Officer Martin.

"I know," said my father. "And I'm glad they've raised the drinking age. Come on, officers, we're not on opposite sides of this one. But I know my daughter and you don't. She doesn't drink. And she hasn't done anything wrong. It's a family matter, and we'll take care of it."

Finally the police officers left. I was relieved but

still scared. The house felt very quiet. I knew I was going to have a lot of explaining to do, and I didn't think that my parents were going to be too happy with what I had to tell them.

THREE

My father poured himself a cup of tea. "Dani, why don't you clean yourself up," he said softly.

"I'm sorry . . . I wasn't drinking . . . I . . ."

"We've already heard what you told the police." He sounded tired. "Go wash up now."

I went into the bathroom. My cheeks had dirt all over them. My hair was sticking out wildly. I washed my face. I still had blood on my jeans from holding the dog, and my sweater reeked of the stuff Michael had spilled on it.

I wondered if Michael was worrying about me? Or about the dog? Or had he passed out somewhere and already forgotten the whole episode? I wondered if he'd remember me in the morning.

I came out of the bathroom. Mom and Dad were sitting on the couch next to each other, talking softly. It was clear that they were talking about me.

"I'm really tired," I said. "I think I'll go to bed now."

"I think there's more for us to discuss," said my father.

"There really isn't any more I can tell you. It wasn't such a big deal."

"Dani," said my mother. "We've always trusted you. Don't you think you should trust us?"

"I told you. I met a guy at Bonnie's party, somebody I know from school, but not real well. He's a senior, and he took driver's ed, so it was legal for him to be driving."

"All right," said my father. "This isn't a court of law, but what happened?"

"*Nothing.*" I wished that I had been able to keep my voice more under control.

"Dani, it's not nothing," said my mother.

"Well, all right, the guy I was with had a little too much to drink. We went out on the highway, just for some air, just like I said, and he hit the dog. Then, when we saw the police, he got scared that he'd be pulled in for drunk driving, so he took off. The rest you know."

"He took off, leaving you in the middle of the highway," said my father. "Some charmer! Who is this creep, Dani?"

I didn't want to have to give my parents Michael's name if I could help it.

My mother interrupted. "Dani, you must have known he was drunk. How could you have been so stupid?"

I shook my head.

"Don't just shake your head like a puppy," said my mother. "You know that drinking and driving are dangerous."

"I know . . . I'm sorry."

"Sorry isn't enough," snapped my mother. "It could have been you lying on that highway, not the dog. How could you be that stupid?"

"Stop calling me stupid," I said. "I'm sorry. What more do you want me to say? *I'm sorry!*"

"I didn't call you stupid, Dani. I called what you did stupid."

"Please, Mom, spare me the psychology. I'd rather you just be mad at me."

"Well, I'm plenty mad," said my mother. "And I do think that you showed shockingly poor judgment. You always said your friends didn't drink. We trusted you, Dani."

"I'm not perfect."

"I'm not worried about your being perfect. I'm worried about your surviving until you're seventeen."

"Dani, your mom's right," my father said. "How could you be so stupid as to go in a car with a guy like that? You said he'd been drinking. In case you've forgotten, it is against the law for teenagers to drink in New Jersey."

"I didn't do anything so terrible," I repeated.

"Dani, don't you see?" pleaded my mother. "It's not what you did. It's what you didn't do. You didn't have the sense not to drive with this boy you knew was drunk."

I shut my mouth. I couldn't explain tonight. How could I tell my parents that even though he was drunk, I still found Michael the most attractive guy I had ever met—the only one who made me feel like a woman.

"Beautiful Daniella," he had said to me under the willow tree in Bonnie's yard. "You look like a Chinese maiden. How come I never noticed how beautiful you are? You must have been avoiding willow trees."

Michael put his arm around my waist and guided me to his car, a Pontiac Trans-AM with an eagle painted across the hood.

"Dani," said my mother. "We're waiting."

I hung my head. After my parents had finally finished their lecture, I went up to my room to bed.

My parents and I usually get along very well. In fact, a lot of kids are jealous of me because they think I never get yelled at.

I lay in my bed, hugging my pillow. I thought of Raynor and Bonnie and the party. Most of all I thought about Michael.

I reached over for my phone. I had to call Bonnie. Not only did my parents think I was stupid, but I had run out on my two best friends when I should have stayed and helped clean up.

The phone at Bonnie's rang and rang. I wondered if the party had completely broken up and if Bonnie was asleep. Or was Bonnie angry at me for just taking off? Maybe she wasn't answering. Finally she picked it up.

"Bonnie," I whispered. "It's me, Dani. I'm home. I didn't mean to just run out on you."

"I was worried about you. I saw you going up the stairs with Michael, and then you just disappeared."

"I know. I'm sorry."

"Stop sounding like I'm your mother. I want to know all the details. Michael Barnard! Did he take you home?"

"Not exactly. Michael ditched me on the highway. The police picked me up."

"What!"

"It's a long story," I said.

"Dani, you sound drunk."

"I'm not. I promise. What a night! I'm sorry I ran out on you."

"This place looks as if we had a roller derby here. Thank goodness my parents are away for the weekend. They'd kill me. Whose idea was it to have this party in the first place?"

"Yours," I reminded Bonnie. "Remember, you

16

said we were sticking to ourselves too much. You said it was time for us to meet new people.''

. ''Well, next time I get an idea like that, stop me. Raynor has passed out on my couch. What should I do with him?''

''You'd better wake him.''

''He looks kind of cute, sleeping,'' said Bonnie.

''Then leave him,'' I said.

Bonnie giggled. ''Maybe I will.''

I heard my parents coming upstairs. ''I've got to go,'' I whispered. ''My folks are mad enough at me. But I didn't give them Michael's name. Thank goodness. They started to ask me who I was with and then they started yelling at me for going driving with someone who was drunk. They'd never let me go out with him again.''

''Did he ask you?''

''No,'' I admitted. But I also had to admit that I wanted to see him again, even after all that had happened.

FOUR

I saw Michael much sooner than I expected. The very next day, in fact. I spent the morning at Bonnie's helping her clean up. In the afternoon I had to go to work at the Pizza Palace. I work there three times a week after school and on Saturday afternoons. I'm trying to save money so I can go away to college.

I was much too tired to work. At least my shift was almost over. Fifteen more minutes and I could go home. Charlie, my boss, noticed that I wasn't being my usual energetic self.

"You look like something the cat dragged in," he said.

"Make it a dog," I said.

"Huh?"

"Never mind. It was a pretty feeble joke."

I was trying to pull mozzarella off a table when a voice behind me made me jump. "Daniella? Our lady of the pizza?"

I spun around to see Michael standing there. He was wearing wraparound shades that looked strange on an early spring day, even though the sun was shining.

"What are you doing here?"

"I stopped at your house and your mom told me that you would be at your job here."

"She wouldn't have been so friendly if she knew who you were."

"Did you get in trouble last night?"

I didn't answer. I scrubbed fiercely at the table. Suddenly I had all my energy back.

"Dani, don't you even want to know why I went to your house?" Michael asked in a teasing voice.

I couldn't believe it. How could Michael just waltz into the Pizza Palace? Of course, Michael had as much of a constitutional right to pizza as anyone, but I didn't want to talk about last night at the place where I worked.

"Excuse me," I said as a dozen kids crowded in. "I've got to wait on customers."

The kids started banging on the table, as if it was a set of drums. They were demanding pizza with pepperoni, repeating "pepperoni" over and over, like a Grand Funk rap.

"Hey, pipe down, shrimps," I shouted. They couldn't have been more than thirteen.

"Pipe-roni . . . pipe-roni," sang one kid in a high, squeaky voice. He got up and danced over to me. Only he wasn't dancing, he was reeling. He was stinking drunk. He tried to make me dance with him.

"Let go of her, kid," said Michael, pulling at the boy's jacket.

"I was just asking for a dance. What's it to you?" The kid shoved Michael. Michael shoved him back. Suddenly three other kids jumped up, knocking over the plastic chairs. Charlie heard the commotion and came running out from behind the counter.

Michael towered over the kid who was flailing at him.

"Hey, cut that out!" shouted Charlie.

Michael was trying to hold off the kid and not hit

him. "Tell this munchkin to let up." Michael grinned at me like the whole thing was a goof. At that moment, the kid saw his chance. He kicked Michael hard, right in the groin. Michael doubled over. Charlie went after the kid who'd kicked Michael. The other kids were making an incredible mess. Chairs and table were overturned. They were throwing hot pepper sauce around.

"Dani, call the police," shouted Charlie.

I ran to the phone and dialed 9II. "There's a fight at the Pizza Palace," I said. The police officer who answered told me someone would be there right away.

I heard the police siren in the distance. The kids heard it, too. One of them shouted, "Hey, let's get out of here."

They were out of sight by the time the police car pulled up. It was the same two officers I had met the night before: Officer Nelson and Officer Martin. They were the last people I wanted to see again. They recognized me right away.

"What's going on?" asked Officer Martin. "We got a nine-one-one here."

"One minute, officer," said Charlie. He went over to thank Michael for helping out. Michael nodded. He couldn't seem to speak yet.

"We were attacked by drunken midgets," said Charlie with a grin. "But they ran out of here when they heard your siren."

"Well, well," said Officer Nelson, giving me a knowing look. "It seems that whenever we meet Miss Nelli, things are a little confusing."

"Dani had nothing to do with this," said Charlie. "She works here. A bunch of kids came in. They must have been all of thirteen. They kicked one of our customers. I tried to stop the fight, and they were all over me. How did it start, Dani?"

The policewoman was looking straight at me. "We meet again," Officer Martin said. She made it sound as if we had a secret relationship.

I swallowed hard.

"Tell the officer what happened, Dani," said Charlie.

"Michael's a friend of mine," I said. "He came in and we were talking, and then those kids came in. They were banging on the table. Then one of them grabbed me, and Michael told him to let go. They all jumped up and Michael got kicked."

"That's when I came into it," said Charlie. "I told Dani to call you. The kids took off."

"They were drunk," I said.

"You seem to be running into a lot of trouble this weekend," Officer Nelson observed.

Both Michael and Charlie stared at me. "I met these two officers last night," I said, throwing Michael a meaningful glance.

Charlie just looked confused. "I'm sorry to have bothered you, officers. There really isn't any damage, except for a few overturned chairs and some sauce thrown around."

"Never underestimate the damage kids can do," Officer Martin said.

"I wonder where kids that age get their hands on liquor?" said Charlie. "Whoever sells it to them should be locked up."

Michael cleared his throat again as if he had something stuck there. "Are you okay?" the policewoman asked him.

Michael nodded.

"How about you, Dani," she asked. "Did those kids hurt you?"

"Just my pride, I guess," I said. "They were so

young. I felt like I should have been able to handle them. I agree with Charlie. Those kids were disgusting."

"I wouldn't go that far," Michael said. "They were just cutting up. They weren't that drunk."

"They stank," I said angrily. "And they were way too young to be drinking."

Officer Nelson stared at me. Then he burst out laughing. "You're not so big yourself," he said.

"I'm sixteen and I'm a sophomore." I pulled up to my full five feet one inch.

Officer Nelson smiled. "Sorry. It's just that you don't look much over thirteen yourself. Too many kids today think that drinking makes them all grown-up. We've got the statistics to show that it can make them dead."

The policeman looked thoughtful. "How is that dog we took to the vet's?"

"I was just going to look in on him on my way home."

"I'll go with you," volunteered Michael. "I'll wait until your quitting time."

"It's past that now," said Charlie. "Dani, thanks for keeping your head. I'm sorry I teased you about being tired today."

The policewoman gave me another one of her significant looks, as if we shared a dirty secret. "Good-bye, Dani," she said. "Try to stay out of trouble for twenty-four hours."

Michael put a protective arm on my elbow.

"Your girlfriend has an unladylike knack for getting herself into trouble," Officer Martin continued.

"Hey, that's sexist," I said.

"You gotta watch yourself with her, officer," said Charlie. "She doesn't take flack from anyone, even a lady cop."

"I don't, either," said Officer Martin, "and I don't like being called a lady cop. Come on, John. I've had enough of kids."

I watched them get back into the police car. I hoped running into them wasn't going to be habit forming.

I turned to Michael. "Wait for me," I said. "I've got to change." I went into the ladies' room and slipped on my jeans and my New York T-shirt with the big purple-glitter letters. My Aunt Robie bought it for me. Ever since I was a baby, she's always given me glitter T-shirts.

I was glad to get out of my uniform. We have to wear these cheap polyester long dresses that push up our busts. We're supposed to look like medieval wenches. I just look silly.

I looked at myself in the mirror. I wished that the police officer hadn't made that crack about my looking thirteen. I ran my fingers through my short hair the way Easton, the guy who cuts it, told me to fluff it. It's supposed to give it a sophisticated punk look. A punk medieval waitress—that's me!

I put on my new lipstick and blotted it so that most of it didn't show. As I went out the door, I remembered what my father had said about Michael: "Some charmer."

He had meant it sarcastically. I shrugged my shoulders and looked at myself again in the mirror. Michael was a charmer. That was the problem.

FIVE

It felt weird to be riding in the front seat of Michael's car again. The whole last twenty-four hours had been weird.

Michael glanced over at me. "You all right?"

"No," I admitted. "It's been a very creepy time. It's enough to make me a fanatic about drinking."

"Aw, come on," said Michael. "I thought it was pretty funny. And I was the one who got kicked. If I can laugh about it, you can."

"Well, I don't think it was a joke. I hated it. I hate drinking. It makes people crazy." I gave him a meaningful look.

"Don't lecture me. I'm sorry I was out of line last night, but I don't drink very much."

I sighed. "Why do you drink at all?" I asked, feeling like a prude, but I meant it. Those thirteen-year-old kids being so high in the middle of the afternoon made me sick.

"Come on, Dani, lighten up," said Michael. "I came over to apologize for the way I acted. I'm really sorry things ended up that way . . . I mean, with you all alone on the highway."

"I wasn't alone. I was with the dog," I said. I stared out the windshield. I didn't feel very comfortable with Michael. I realized we didn't have any friends in common. How could we? I didn't have any friends outside of my class. Michael was the first senior I had ever been alone with.

"Dani, it's not like you to be so quiet."

"You don't really know what I'm like and vice versa. I was just thinking about how little we knew each other. All I know is that you've read a lot about Vietnam."

"Well, how was I supposed to get to know you? At school you always march around in a group. You and Raynor and Bonnie are together every moment. I never see you alone."

I thought about it. In school, Raynor, Bonnie, and I did always meet after every class. How many kids had I turned off because I was never alone?

"Do you spend much time alone?" I asked.

Michael nodded. "Yeah, I always have. Maybe because I'm an only child."

"But I'm an only child, too. Besides, you're so popular," I blurted out.

"Thanks," Michael said. "Yeah, I got lots of friends, but I don't have one or two really close ones like you do."

"I feel strange talking to you like this, when we don't know each other very well."

"How do you think people get to know each other?" Michael smiled at me.

When we drove into Dr. Vickers's driveway, I flashed to an instant replay of the previous night. We went in without saying a word. The door to the clinic was open. I could hear a phone ringing in the back. Michael looked nervous. He was so easy to read. His face wasn't just handsome. He had one of the most expressive faces I had ever seen. He surprised me. It was as if I didn't expect to see such a flickering of expressions on a handsome guy.

Dr. Vickers came out. She smiled wide when she saw me. She has a little gap in her front teeth that makes her look like Lauren Hutton.

"Hi, Dani. Here to check on your patient? I've got good news for you."

"You mean the dog is going to live?" Said Michael in an incredulous voice. "I figured he was a goner."

"No, he was just in shock. He's in pretty good shape, except for a nasty scrape on his belly. Would you like to see him? He's got a sweet nature."

The noise in the back of the office was incredible—most of it coming from a large golden retriever with a wide white bandage around its middle. The bandage gave the animal a curiously bisected look. The dog was barking furiously, and each of its barks was answered by a shrill bark from a little terrier.

I looked in the cages for what I was already beginning to think of as "my" dog. "Where is he?" I asked.

Dr. Vickers laughed. "You'll never guess. It's the golden retriever. He just looked black from all the grease on him."

"Do you remember me?" I knelt beside the dog's cage and held out my hand in a closed fist. My fingers curled up, so that he would know that I wasn't trying to grab him. That was the way Dr. Vickers had told me to approach an animal that doesn't know you.

The dog moved forward in his cage and sniffed my hand. Very slowly his tail began to wag. Michael knelt beside me. The dog's tongue reached through the cage and licked Michael's knuckle.

"Can we take him out of his cage?" I asked.

"Sure," said Dr. Vickers. "He could use a walk. Except for the bruises he's a very healthy dog. I wonder why someone would just abandon him?"

She unlatched the cage, and the dog stepped out with a dignified air. He wagged his tail vigorously as Michael bent down and patted him, scratching one ear and then the other.

When we were outside, the dog sniffed the fresh air with his nose high, reminding me of a prisoner who had just been given a reprieve. He tugged at his leash.

I started to run with him.

"Do you want me to take him?" Michael asked.

"No—"

"Please, I want to."

Reluctantly I handed the leash over to Michael.

"What's the matter?"

"Last night, you wanted to leave this dog to die. I thought you didn't like dogs," I said.

"You mean, because I run them over?" The bitterness in Michael's voice surprised me.

"No, I wasn't thinking that. I know that was an accident, only—"

"Only I was drunk and left him to die on the highway. I could have gotten us both killed. You've been thinking about it the whole time I've been with you. I could tell."

"Well, it's not something I can forget very easily."

"I haven't forgotten it, either. Look, I came to see you because I couldn't get last night out of my mind."

"Me, or the accident?"

"Both."

"It wasn't an accident. If you hadn't been drinking, it would never have happened."

"You can't know that."

I shook my head stubbornly. "I hope you'll think about that *accident*, Michael. I hope you'll think about it the next time you want a drink."

Michael snorted. "You sound like you're from the Salvation Army. I expect you to start saving my soul any minute."

"I wouldn't do that."

"Why not?" Michael grinned at me. "It might be fun."

"You're making fun of me now. I can't help it if I was raised by a pair of do-gooders. Ever since I was a tiny kid, they've drummed it into me that you should do what you think is right." I stopped.

"What's wrong?" Michael asked.

"Well, my parents don't think I did the right thing last night."

"Do you always do what your parents tell you to do?"

"No. I didn't tell them your name, for one thing. And they didn't make me tell the police about you. My parents aren't so bad. They aren't your typical do-gooders. They believe in having fun."

"You sound like you and your folks get along."

"We do . . . except for last night."

"I already said I was sorry," said Michael.

"I know. Let's not talk about it anymore. Let's just drop it."

"Okay," said Michael. We stood around awkwardly for a few seconds. Neither of us could think of anything to say.

"What do you think is going to happen to this dog?" Michael asked, as glad as I was to change the subject. "Do you think you'll ever find the real owners?"

"Me . . . why me?"

Michael looked a little embarrassed. "I don't know. It just seems like the kind of thing you would do. Either find the real owner or make sure the dog gets a good home."

"Dr. Vickers will have to take him to the pound. My mom says we already have enough strays. We have two cats we adopted. Or, rather, they adopted us." Michael made me mad. He just assumed that Ms. Too-Good-to-Be-Believed would take care of the dog.

"What'll happen to him at the pound?"

"He'll probably have to be destroyed, so you don't have to feel guilty about running him over."

The dog was sniffing around in the dirt. "You mean that this beautiful dog is a stray? Didn't he have a collar and a license on him or anything?"

I shook my head, feeling much less angry. "Dr. Vickers says that a lot of dogs are abandoned on the highway. People just pull over to the side, let the dogs out the door, and forget about them."

"I bet they don't forget about them," Michael said softly. "I bet they remember and feel guilty for a long time." He bent down and called the dog to him. "Here, boy, come here, Tequila."

"Why do you call him that?"

"Cause that's what I was drinking when we met. Besides, he looks like Tequila Gold." The dog licked his hand as if he liked his new name.

"Tell you what, Tequila," Michael said. "You get better, and you can have a home with me. I've never had a pet."

"Can you really take him?" I asked. "Will your

parents let you keep a dog now if they never let you before?''

Michael looked at me as if I were loony. "I just never asked for one before," he said.

"And you can just get whatever you ask for?"

Michael laughed. "Stop looking at me as if I'm nuts.''

"It's not that. I don't know. It just seems like you're adopting this dog on a whim.''

"You were the one who told me he'd be destroyed if you didn't find a good home for him. What's the matter? Don't you think I'll give him a good home?''

"Well, you've never taken care of a dog before. It's a lot of work.''

"I'm not afraid of the work. What are *you* afraid of, Dani?''

I couldn't answer him.

SIX

About a week later the doorbell rang and Officer John Nelson was standing on our front porch. He looked a little hesitant, as if I wouldn't remember him. But I did. He was still the cutest police officer I had ever seen.

"Hello, Dani. Are your parents home?"

Funny how my heart started thumping when he asked that question, even though I hadn't done anything wrong. My parents were home. My father was just about to make fettuccine in his pasta machine.

I heard my father shout from the kitchen, "Dani! We're about to start. Get in here. And if that's Raynor and Bonnie, bring 'em along."

"It's a police officer, Dad."

I heard the pasta machine start up, and I knew my father hadn't heard me. "Mom and Dad are in the kitchen," I said to Officer Nelson. "You'd better come with me."

"Thanks," said Officer Nelson. He coughed. "Dani, I'm really not here for . . . it's nothing terrible," he said.

His words didn't reassure me. My dad looked startled when we walked into the kitchen. He was wearing jeans and a TREVIRA TWOSOME TEN MILE

31

T-shirt. He likes to eat so much that he still has a belly, even with all his running.

"I'm sorry to disturb you when you're in the middle of fixing dinner," Officer Nelson said.

My father put down the measuring cup of flour he was holding. "I think you'd better tell us the reason for your visit, officer. The last time we saw you was not a happy occasion."

"Let me assure you, Mr. Nelli. It's nothing like that. I decided to come over rather than telephoning because I was in the neighborhood, and I thought you would all want to hear about this. Dani and you."

I got very nervous when I heard my name.

"We're starting a new program," explained Officer Nelson. "The DA wants to crack down on liquor stores that sell to kids. I've been impressed by Dani, and I know she comes from a family that believes in community service. I'd like Dani to be a volunteer. She'd be working with us undercover."

"Dani! An undercover agent!" My father almost fell into his pasta machine.

Officer Nelson looked at me and my mother for approval before going on. "It would take our entire force to stake out all the liquor stores in town. We've had severe budget cuts. We just can't do it. A teenage volunteer could help us. We'd give her money to buy booze. A police officer would go with her, of course—an undercover cop. We know of towns in New York where they've tried programs like this and gotten good results. I was asked to suggest a trustworthy teenager for the program. We want to start out with just one, as a pilot project. And we don't want to use anyone connected with the police. I thought of Dani right away." Officer Nelson turned to my father. "I know your reputation around city hall as a pretty straight shooter. No one would suspect Dani of working undercover with the police. I thought your daughter would be perfect, if she was interested.''

The silence in our kitchen felt as if a weight had descended. I closed my mouth, having only then realized it had been hanging open.

"You were right, Officer Nelson," said my father. "It certainly wasn't what we expected."

"I can't believe you thought of *me!*" I said.

"I remembered what you said in the Pizza Palace the other day," Officer Nelson said.

I remembered how Michael had gotten mad at me for saying that kids who drank were disgusting. Well, too bad. Nothing I did or said was going to make Michael want to take me out, anyway. Michael had adopted Tequila, but that seemed to be the limit of our relationship. Occasionally, he would stop me on the way to class to ask me about Tequila's diet or exercise, as if I were the animal expert. Or he would call me at home to talk about Tequila, but he never suggested we get together. The only time I saw him outside of school was when he had to take Tequila to Dr. Vickers for some shots. He stopped over to say hello, but he didn't stay long. I wondered if he thought that I was just too much of a prude, that I had sounded like I was from the Salvation Army. If he had wanted to see me alone, he would have had no problem.

Bonnie and Raynor and I seemed to be out of sync all of a sudden, too. Nothing I could put my finger on, but something was just not quite right.

Perhaps that explains why I was so flattered that at least Officer Nelson remembered and thought well of me.

"Well," said Officer Nelson. "I know this comes as a surprise, but what do you think?"

"I'm interested," I said quickly.

"Not so fast," said my mother. "This is a lot to digest. I think we all have a million questions to ask. Why don't you stay and have dinner?"

"But I have to tell you from the start that I don't like entrapment and I don't like the idea of Dani's being mixed up in anything dangerous," said my father, as if I hadn't just said I was interested. He made me mad.

"It shouldn't be dangerous," said Officer Nelson. "It's not a violent crime we're talking about, and a police officer will be nearby at all times."

"Come on, Dani. Let's make some pasta for the officer," said my father. We all sat down at the big oak table in our kitchen. "In this family we don't talk about anything without eating," said my father.

"I want to know why you thought of me." I blurted out. "You don't really know me."

"Well, I've seen the way you handled yourself in two emergencies. You didn't panic in either of them."

"Dani's a pretty levelheaded kid," my mother agreed.

I felt flattered and excited. This was much better than being picked for something by a teacher— someone from the outside, Officer Nelson, had seen me in action and he liked what he saw.

And I liked Officer Nelson. It would serve Michael right if I became an undercover agent and he couldn't buy booze anymore. Officer Nelson thought I was special. That was more than Michael thought.

"What would I be doing exactly?"

"Well, first, you and your parents would come down and talk to the DA. Basically we'd want you to go into stores and try to buy liquor. We'd have a plainclothes officer to observe the buy. We'd keep track of liquor stores that didn't ask you for an ID. Then the DA could go after an indictment. You'd work after school and on Saturdays.''

"But I already work," I said.

"If you did this," said my mother, "and I am saying 'if,' Dani, you might have to arrange a break from the Pizza Palace. How long would this program last?''

"Not more than a few weeks. The hard part is that it must be kept absolutely secret. You won't be able to tell your friends what you're doing, Dani.''

Right now that didn't look like too much of a problem. My friends didn't seem too friendly, anyhow.

I liked the idea that I would work secretly. No one would know what I was doing. Nobody would be able to tease me about being a goody-two-shoes. And I would be doing something to stop other kids from drinking.

Best of all, it sounded exciting. It would be my secret. "Would I be working with you, Officer Nelson?" I asked. I remembered the way he had knelt beside me next to Tequila. He wasn't really old, for a police officer. And he was so handsome. The thought that we would be working together made me happy.

"Call me John. That's the plan. You would be working with my partner and myself. We'll give you some training, tell you what to expect. You're smart. You'll pick things up fast.''

I liked that he thought I was smart. "I think I'd like to try it," I said.

"Wait a minute, Dani," said my dad. "I have a lot more questions.''

This was my decision. Officer John Nelson had come to *me*, because he saw something special in me.

My father caught my expression. "Take that frown off your face, Dani, and hear me out. I have a few questions about entrapment. That's what she would be doing, wouldn't she, officer?"

"Technically, it's entrapment."

"Let's take a hypothetical example," said my father in his lawyer voice. "Somebody owns a liquor store. As far as we know, this owner has no intention or pattern of selling to minors. Dani walks in. She has a winning manner. She's polite. The owner or clerk sells her a bottle of booze. It's true the owner has broken the law, but would he have if Dani hadn't offered the temptation?"

Officer Nelson listened to my father's argument with his lips drawn together. "If you want my opinion," he said, sounding angry, "yes, your hypothetical owner would have broken the law, if not with Dani, then with some other minor, and that minor might just get into a car and kill someone. Nobody's holding a gun to the owner's head, saying sell liquor to Dani. The owner should ask for an ID, and if Dani doesn't have one, he should throw her out of the store. Your daughter doesn't even look sixteen, much less twenty-one. You can't put handcuffs on the police all the time, Mr. Nelli. We can't stake out liquor stores and wait for minors to happen to go in and make a buy. We just don't have enough officers to go around—not to do our job properly—and protect people against more violent crimes. But teenage drinking is a serious problem. Talk to someone whose child has been killed by a drunk teenager. We've raised the drinking age; we have a tough new drunk-driving law. But if we can't enforce the new laws, we're back to square one." He looked at me. "I'm sorry. I didn't mean to sound like I was giving you a lecture."

"Join the club," I said.

"Excuse me?"

"Nothing. It's just that I get accused of giving lectures by my friends, especially about drinking."

My father still looked worried. "Dani, I want you to think about this before we make a decision."

"But it is *my* decision, dad."

"I'm sure the police won't let you do it unless we approve," said my mother.

"Of course," said Officer Nelson. "You'll have to sign a release."

"But I should have the final say," I argued. "I wouldn't be doing anything wrong. I'd be doing something right!"

"I know that's what you believe, Dani," said my father. "But . . ."

"No buts. You said I showed poor judgment the night Officer Nelson brought me home. Well, now I'm going to do something about it. You should be glad."

"I'm glad that you want to do something, but I'm not sure that this is what you should be doing."

"How can I learn to have good judgment if you don't give me a chance to use my own?"

"It's just that—"

"Just that you think I should always agree with you," I said angrily.

My father shook his head. "Dani, no, no. . . . Is that what you think?"

It didn't seem fair. I wanted my parents to think it was terrific that the police had thought of me for their program and to think I was terrific for wanting to volunteer.

"What do you think, Mom?" I asked. "You've been awfully quiet."

"Well, I have mixed feelings. I'm proud of you, of course, proud that Officer Nelson thought of you. I understand how Dad feels about entrapment, but I'm not sure that he's right. I don't think there was any way in the world that those congressmen who were eager to take bribes would have been caught if the FBI hadn't tried something like "Abscam." Some crimes are just too difficult to discover without something like entrapment. And I think selling liquor to minors is in that category. I'm sorry, Ed, I disagree with you. Dani, I think it's going to have to be your decision."

My father looked at Officer Nelson. "Tell me, if you weren't a police officer, and Dani were your daughter, would you want her to be involved?"

Officer Nelson studied his plate as if it held the secrets of the universe. "Honestly, I can't see how this program could be dangerous. If she were my daughter, I think I would want her to make up her own mind."

My father sighed. "This still makes me uneasy. But, all right, Dani, it's up to you."

"I want to do it," I said. "I want to volunteer."

I knew my motives weren't the purest. I wanted to prove to my parents that I did have good judgment. I wanted to show Michael, sort of paying him back for not asking me out. And I did it because Officer Nelson was cute.

And after everything that happened, I still don't know if it was a good thing that I volunteered.

SEVEN

The day of my first undercover assignment I was nervous from the minute I woke up. I must have slept nervous. Even the cats noticed. Ringo, our long-haired cat, usually sleeps with me, but I rolled around so much during the night that when I woke up I saw him staring at me from the chair next to my bed. He gave me a look as if he couldn't believe that I could be so rude.

I couldn't decide what to wear. I had been told to wear my regular clothes. Did regular mean I should wear jeans and a sweater, or could I wear a mini-skirt? I have good legs. It's the one advantage of being flat chested and skinny. I decided to wear my red-and-white striped mini. My Aunt Robie bought it for me. She always gets me the neatest stuff. I looked at myself in the mirror. I just hoped I didn't look like a barber pole.

When I got to school that morning, Michael asked me where the party was. "Am I invited?"

"No party," I answered.

"You're all dressed up."

"Oh, this," I said blushing. "I just felt like wearing it."

"Well, it looks good."

This was the first time he had talked to me and not

mentioned Tequila. Maybe he would finally ask me out. But he just gave me a high sign, turned on his heel, and left me standing there. I wondered what he'd think if he knew what I was going to do that afternoon.

Bonnie tapped me on the shoulder. "What are you all dressed up for?" she asked.

I looked down at myself. "It's just my regular clothes."

Bonnie looked me over. "That's your good mini-skirt," she said.

"I know," I admitted. "I just woke up feeling depressed this morning and felt like wearing it, to lighten up."

Bonnie looked sympathetic, and I felt bad that I was having to lie to her. "Why were you feeling so low?"

I shrugged. "It just seems like everything's different lately." Just then Raynor came over. He and Bonnie glanced at each other. They looked guilty about something, but I couldn't figure out what. Maybe it wasn't them. Maybe I was feeling guilty for keeping secrets.

"Dani's depressed," said Bonnie.

"It's no big deal," I said.

"Let's all get together tonight," said Raynor. "We haven't hung out, just the three of us, in a while."

"Great idea," said Bonnie. Her voice sounded a shade too enthusiastic.

I thought quickly. I was supposed to meet the police at four o'clock. In theory, I'd be finished by dinner. I hoped my assignment wouldn't run late. "Let's meet at my house," I said. It would be weird to be with my two best friends and not talk about my afternoon.

"Sure," said Raynor.

We headed for our next class. I had Spanish and I knew they both had physics. We separated and I watched them go down the hall, whispering to each other. Their heads were close together. I wished that I hadn't told them I was feeling low. In fact, I was feeling excited.

I had been told to meet the police officers in Bingham Park after school. It's right down the hill from the high school. John said that he and his partner would be in street clothes. I almost didn't recognize them out of uniform. Officer Martin was wearing jeans, and she had heavy legs that looked even bigger in tight jeans than when she was in uniform.

But John looked even better out of uniform. He had on a blue crew-neck sweater. The blue was lighter than his eyes, and he had on gray polished cotton pants. He looked preppie. His hair looked much cuter without a hat on it. I wondered if he had a girlfriend.

He nodded when he saw me. "You look good," he said.

Officer Martin looked me over. "She looks too conspicuous," she said.

I felt so embarrassed. "You told me to wear my regular clothes. Well, these *are* my regular clothes."

"The miniskirt makes her look a little older," John said. "It's no problem. But, Dani, there's been a slight change of plans. You'll be working with Officer Martin today."

I tried not to show my disappointment, but I wanted to cry. Half of my reason for volunteering was that I wanted to work with John. I didn't even like Officer

Martin, and for some reason I was scared to be alone with her.

John gave me a reassuring smile. "This is only for today. Okay, I have the money." He reached into his pocket and brought out a fat roll of bills. He peeled off fifty dollars and gave it to me. His roll of bills still looked fat.

Officer Martin frowned at me when I shoved the money into a pocket of my skirt. "Don't lose that," she said. "Our budget is very tight these days. We don't have much of that green stuff to throw around."

"I'm not gonna lose it," I said defensively. She made me feel like a little kid again.

"Put it in your knapsack," she said, as if it were an order. I obeyed.

John gave me another smile, as if trying to tell me not to let her bother me. "Good luck, Dani." I liked the way my name sounded when he spoke it.

I smiled at him. I wanted it to be a jaunty smile— the smile of a resistance fighter going out and facing death. Of course, I knew I wasn't facing death and I wasn't a resistance fighter, but that's the kind of smile I wanted.

Officer Martin's car was a white Corvette.

"Is this yours?" I asked, surprised.

She smiled at me for the first time, a genuine smile, and it changed her whole face. "Like it?" she asked.

"It's incredible."

She opened the door and slipped behind the wheel. I hurried to the other side and got in. The car had that new-car smell that I wish could be bottled. The dashboard looked like something out of a *Star Wars* movie, like it was supposed to control a missile, not a car.

"Is it brand-new?" I asked.

"I've had it a few months, but I'm still learning about it. It's a terrific machine. This car practically drives itself by computer. It tells you how many miles of gas you've got left; it even tells you the temperature outside. Push that top button." She pointed to a panel of about a dozen black buttons.

I pushed the one that said TEM and a digital display showed "58" in red lights. "Amazing," I said.

"That's nothing. I think this car could write out parking tickets if I programmed it right. It's a mean machine." She laughed again.

I laughed with her. "It's great. Somehow it wasn't the car I expected you to be driving."

"People don't expect women to want powerful cars."

"I think women look great in sports cars, especially behind the wheel."

"You know, that's not a bad line. I may use it myself, but I'll give you credit."

"Thanks, Officer Martin."

"If we're going to be working together, you can call me Jessica."

Her name was a surprise, too. I had imagined her being called something like Maude or Henrietta. Jessica is one of my favorite names.

"What did you think—that I was named Harold?" Her laugh was more of a bark.

"No, no. It's just that I would have liked to be named Jessica myself, if I could have picked."

"But we can't always pick, can we?" she said. She seemed to be talking about more than just names.

We drove through the Hollow, a rundown part of town. The white Corvette got a few stares from guys hanging around the street corners. "Aren't you afraid to drive through here with this car?" I asked.

She laughed that barking laugh again. "Are you kidding? Remember, I carry a gun."

I knew she was tough. She didn't have to prove it to me.

"Do you like being a police officer?" I asked.

"It has its compensations," she said.

"Like what?"

"You're persistent, aren't you?"

"Well, I really want to know," I said.

She laughed, but I didn't know what she was laughing about. "Well, you're probably expecting me to tell you that police work isn't very glamorous. The truth is that you get to spend a fair amount of time by yourself, which I like. You get to poke into other's people business, which I like. You get respect, which I like, even if it's just that people are afraid of you."

I didn't know how to take her speech. It sounded as if she liked being a cop because it made her feel macho and it did something for her ego. I wasn't sure that was the best reason to be a cop. But then, I wasn't sure that I had agreed to volunteer as an undercover agent for very good reasons, either.

We drove out of the Hollow and up to the Village Green. Jessica parked her car expertly. I wished that I could park that well. I flunked my first driving test.

"Here we are," Jessica said. "Are you ready for your first collar?"

"Collar?"

"Just police slang. If we bust the owner, I'll share the credit with you."

"But . . . we're not going to arrest anyone today,"

44

I said. The thought that she might make an arrest my first time out frightened me half to death.

"I'm only kidding. Dani, if you're going to be involved in police work at all, you're going to have to keep your sense of humor. No one can survive in this business without it."

"Most people think I have a good sense of humor." I knew my voice sounded squeaky. Bragging about my sense of humor was about the most humorless thing I could think of.

Jessica looked at me as if I were a twit, and I couldn't blame her. Now that I thought I liked her, I wanted her to like me, too. "Let's go, kiddo," she said. "You go in there and try to make a buy."

"Where will you be?" I asked.

"I'll be around, don't worry. I'll see you when you come out."

I got out of the Corvette. I tugged at my miniskirt and felt the pile of bills in my knapsack. I swallowed hard and tried to tell myself that I had no reason to be nervous. I knew I was lying.

EIGHT

A bell rang over the door as I entered the liquor store. The man behind the counter looked up. He had bulging eyes behind thick glasses. The store was empty. I saw a display of the cans of sweet drinks that I knew a lot of kids liked.

"Excuse me," I said. "Can you help me?"

"What do you think—I'm here for my health?" He stared down at me. His eyes were locked on my bust. What a slimy guy!

"Can I have two piña coladas?"

"A sweet drink for a sweet girl. Is one for me, sweetie?"

"No, one's not for you," I said through gritted teeth.

"I was only teasing you, sweetheart. What's the matter? Don't you have a sense of humor?"

I wanted to punch him. I was sure he would sell me liquor even if I was ten years old. I was glad that I was working with the police. I looked forward to the moment when he learned that I was an undercover agent and we closed him down.

"You know, cutie," he said. "Your eyes flash when you're mad. Does your boyfriend ever tell you that?"

"None of your business," I said icily. "Would you just give me the piña coladas, please?"

He folded his hands across his chest and grinned at me. He was really enjoying himself. "One minute, honey. I don't come across for nothing. I want to see your ID."

I shrugged my shoulders. "I forgot it," I said. "I just ran out without my purse."

"You know the law, sweetie. You wouldn't want me to get in trouble, would you?"

I shook my head. I felt like this guy was toying with me, the way our cats would toy with a bug. Could he possibly know why I was there?

"No ID, no cocktails. Come back when you're a few years older," he said as I left.

I could feel myself blushing a deep red. Jessica was on the corner. She turned when she saw my reflection in a store window. "What's the matter?" she asked. "You look the color of those stripes on your skirt."

"He was a creep," I said. "But he asked for my ID."

Jessica laughed. "You're not supposed to be disappointed because someone is law-abiding," she said.

"I know, but he kept making all these sexist cracks."

"Welcome to the real world of police work. It means being able to tolerate a lot of put-downs and a lot of dead ends. I hope John didn't sell you a bill of goods on police work. Let me give you a warning—take everything John Nelson says with a grain of salt. You're just a volunteer. You can quit anytime."

"I'm not going to quit," I said. "Let's go to the next store on the list. Maybe my sense of humor isn't as good as I thought, but I'm not a quitter."

We went into the next place on the list—the Grog and Grape, a much classier-looking store. It had barrels of wine on display. I was sure that they, too, would ask me for my ID.

The clerk was a blond guy in his early twenties. All his clothes looked like they had just come back from the cleaners. An old guy in front of me bought a half-pint of vodka. I didn't think he had much money, and he seemed to be spending the last of it on booze.

"Can I help you, miss?" the clerk said.

"I'd like tequila," I said.

"Brand?"

I scanned the shelves quickly. I didn't know any brand names for tequila. Then I remembered something Michael had said: "Tequila Gold."

The clerk got a bottle down from a high shelf. I almost gasped when I saw the price. It was twenty dollars, almost half of my expense account for the day. I should have asked for something cheaper. But I didn't want to make a fool of myself by asking for something else.

I held my breath waiting for his next words. "Will that be all?" he asked.

I nodded. I took out the crumpled dollars from the pocket of my knapsack. He wrapped up the bottle. No questions asked. I couldn't wait to get outside and show Jessica my bottle.

"Have a nice day," the clerk said politely.

"You, too," I managed, hoping that my voice sounded normal.

Jessica came into the liquor store just as I was leaving. She saw the brown bag and gave me a nod. Was Jessica going to confront the clerk? Instead, she went to the counter, then slapped her pocket. "Son of a gun," she said. "Forgot my wallet. I'll be right back."

She rushed past me out the door. Around the corner where the Corvette was parked, she cocked a finger at me as if it were a gun. "Bull's eye, kid. I see you scored."

"But what were you doing in the liquor store? I almost dropped the bottle when I saw you."

"You were in there a long time. I began to get worried. This is the first time I've ever had to work with a civilian."

"I did okay," I said. "You don't have to worry about me."

"Get in the car," she said. "And we'll dictate some notes."

I got in the front seat. My feeling of triumph left me as Jessica filled out the form, name of shop, street address, name of agent (that was me). She smiled when I told her that I had bought Tequila Gold.

"Expensive taste."

"Yeah, I didn't realize it cost so much."

"Okay, Dani," Jessica said. "Let's go and see what other villains we can catch today. Only next time, try to make the funds last."

"Do you think this program is a waste of time?"

"Why do you ask that?"

"Because of the sarcastic way you said 'other villains.' You sound like you think we should leave the liquor-store owners alone."

"Well, I'm not sure I think selling to minors is the worst crime on the books. But look, you're saving me time."

Somehow I wanted to be doing something more important than just saving her time.

By the end of the afternoon, I felt I could walk into any liquor store in town and buy anything I wanted. Only one other clerk had asked for my ID. Behind the seats, the Corvette was stuffed with booze. It was all evidence, each piece labeled by Jessica. It would end up in a locked room in the municipal building, waiting until I had to appear before a grand jury and give my testimony.

NINE

Raynor sprawled on our living-room couch, his legs resting on Bonnie's lap. He leaned over and said something to her.

"What's that?" I asked.

Bonnie blushed.

"Nothing," said Raynor quickly, dragging out the word. It was the first time that I could remember being with Bonnie and Raynor when we had to search for conversation. Bonnie and Raynor kept looking at each other as if they didn't want me to be mad at them.

I was dying to tell them about my afternoon with Jessica, but I had promised that I wouldn't tell anyone. Now that the three of us were together again, I hated having secrets. Yet neither Bonnie nor Raynor acted as if they realized that I had something to hide. I decided that I must be a much better actress than I realized. We played some records and talked about school, but it all felt like kid stuff after what had happened with Jessica.

I was trying to think of something to say when the doorbell rang. The three of us were alone in the house. My mom and dad had gone to a party. I wasn't expecting anyone.

"I'll get it," Raynor said.

"It's Dani's house," said Bonnie.

The doorbell rang again. "Somebody'd better get that," I said. "Go on, Raynor . . ."

Neither Bonnie nor I said anything after Raynor went to the door. The seconds felt like minutes, because Bonnie and I were always chattering away together.

"I'm sorry," said Bonnie, so softly that at first I didn't hear her.

"What's going on with you and Raynor?" I said. "It's weird."

Bonnie wouldn't look at me. "Uh . . . nothing."

"Hello," said a voice that made me jump up. It was Michael. Tequila was on a leash at his side, wagging his tail. Raynor was standing behind them.

I had no idea what Michael was doing at my house. "Do you know Bonnie Hoffman?"

"I don't think we were formally introduced, but I crashed your party a while ago. I guess I owe you an apology. I ought to thank you, too. If it hadn't been for your party, I'd never have met Tequila here." Michael looked at me. "And Dani," he added. *As an afterthought?*

Raynor coughed. "Look, Bonnie and I had better be going," he said. "We've got to split."

"I didn't mean to break things up," said Michael.

"Come on, Raynor, don't leave," I pleaded. I wanted Michael to get to know Raynor and Bonnie. I thought it would help make everything more comfortable.

"No, we've got to be going," said Raynor, as if he and Bonnie were an old couple. Suddenly I wondered. Was something romantic going on between Bonnie and Raynor? Ever since the party, the two of

52

them had seemed closer to each other than to me, but I had chalked it up to my being involved, sort of, with Michael. Bonnie stood up. "I'll call you in the morning," she said.

" 'Bye, Dani," said Raynor. "Have a good evening." He winked at me.

"I'll see you to the door" I said. I couldn't resist the desire to poke him one.

"Hey," said Raynor.

"You deserve it."

"Huh? I thought we were doing you a favor, leaving you alone with lover boy."

"He's not my lover boy. We've never even had a date."

"Yeah, well, he sure acts like he's at home here."

"He only stops by now and then when he's walking Tequila."

"Well, now's your chance," said Raynor.

"Raynor, stop it. How come you two are going so soon? I really wish you'd stay."

Raynor and Bonnie exchanged glances. "Come on, Dani, admit it," said Bonnie. "You want to be alone with Michael."

I blushed. "Well . . ."

"So have a good time. You're old enough to take care of yourself," said Raynor. "That's what you told me the night of Bonnie's party."

"It's not what my parents think."

"At least he's not driving tonight," said Raynor. "Go on, he's gonna think you deserted him."

Part of me wanted to hold onto Bonnie and Raynor and part of me wanted to rush back to Michael. I let them go. Bonnie gave me a sympathetic look, as if she were sorry that they were going. But she didn't say, "Raynor, let's stay."

Michael was half sprawled on the couch with Tequila on his chest, licking his face. Tequila jumped off the couch and came over to me.

"Fickle hound!" said Michael. He grinned at me and patted the couch. "Come on, sit down. You look sad—a little bit like you lost your best friend."

"I feel a little like that," I admitted.

"I didn't interrupt an argument, did I?" asked Michael.

I shook my head. "No . . . it's just been weird around here lately—I mean, between Bonnie and Raynor and me. I don't know what it is."

Michael put his arm around me. "Come here," he said. "I have something that will help."

I laughed. "What's that?"

"Close your eyes," said Michael. "It's a surprise."

I closed my eyes. When I felt Michael's lips on mine, I jumped. I'm so dumb I hadn't even expected him to kiss me. His lips felt wonderful—not soft and squishy but not too hard, either.

But I could smell liquor on his breath. I pulled away a little.

"Have you been drinking?" I asked.

"What's the matter? I'm not driving tonight. You and Tequila taught me better than that."

"Thanks."

Michael looked hurt. "I meant it as a compliment. You and Tequila are the two most sober beings I know. I respect you both for it."

"He's a dog, Michael. I'm a person."

"A girl, Dani," said Michael. "Almost a woman. I haven't forgotten."

My heart felt as if it were taking a high dive from the forty-meter board. "You'd better go," I said.

54

"Go on, Michael. You and Tequila go home and sleep it off."

I wanted Michael to say, "Hey, Dani, I'm not drunk. I came over because I wanted to see you." But, instead, he pulled himself off the couch. "You're right," he said. "It wouldn't look right for me to pass out here."

I felt like crying. I wanted Bonnie and Raynor to be my best friends again, and I wanted Michael to want me all the time, not just when he was drunk.

TEN

On my next assignment I got my wish! John Nelson was assigned to me. He drove an old Plymouth Valiant that looked as if he'd had it since high school.

Our hands touched when John and I both put on our seat belts at the same time, and he quickly pulled away from me. Did he think I had deliberately tried to hold his hand? A kid with a crush?

I tried to make conversation, but everytime I spoke, he cut me off curtly. I couldn't understand it. He was acting as if he were mad at me. I hadn't done anything.

We drove in silence the rest of the way to the first liquor store on our list. "You know the routine," he said. "I'll be nearby."

"Where exactly?" I asked. "Jessica always waits for me where I can see her."

"Don't tell me how to do my job, please, Dani."

"I'm sorry. It's just . . . did I do anything to make you mad?"

"Of course not," he snapped. "You're being supersensitive."

Naturally, that only made me feel worse. I got out of the car with a bad feeling. Before I had felt bad that I had to work with Jessica, but now that I was working with John, I didn't like it at all.

The liquor store sold me a bottle of rum without

any problem. The guy even gave me a recipe for piña coladas. John took the bottle, but he wasted no extra words on me. It was like that all afternoon, very businesslike, but it certainly wasn't fun. In fact, it was kind of chilling.

Our last stop was the Grog and Grape. "Make it snappy," said John, as he parked. "After this, we're both off duty." He sounded as if he couldn't wait.

"I'll try," I said. "I see you're in a hurry."

"Dani, I'm sorry if I've been short tempered today. It's got nothing to do with you. I've got a lot on my mind."

I hesitated with my hand on the car door. I wanted him to say more. But all he said was, "Go on." At least he didn't sound angry anymore.

As I stepped out, I saw a golden retriever tied to a bike rack. It got up and wagged its tail hard. "Tequila?" I said. "What are you doing here?" Tequila only wagged his tail harder.

Michael was just coming out of the liquor store with a package under his arm.

"Dani?" he looked surprised.

"Hi," I answered weakly.

"What are you doing here?"

"I was just walking by. I saw Tequila." I couldn't tell Michael that I was trying to gather evidence that the Grog and Grape sold to minors. Michael himself was the proof. And I couldn't go into the store now. Michael was sure to suspect something. I glanced toward John's car. He was pretending to read a newspaper, but I saw his head turn toward me.

"Come on," Michael said. "My errands are done. I'll walk you home."

"Uhh . . ."

Michael looked down at the package in his hand.

57

"Oh . . . I get it. You're mad because I was buying liquor. Believe it or not, it wasn't for me. It's for a friend of mine, but I suppose by your standards that's just as bad. Anyhow, the guy who works here is my cousin. To tell you the truth, he's not too swift. That's one reason I come here. I don't even think he can add to twenty-one."

The fact that Michael knew the clerk, that he was his *cousin*, only made things worse. Tequila tugged at his leash. Michael put his arm around my shoulder. "You look like finding me coming out of a liquor store is the greatest tragedy in the world."

"Wait a minute," I said. I ducked under Michael's arm. "A friend of my family drove me here. I've got to tell him I'm walking home."

I hoped Michael wouldn't recognize John from the Pizza Palace. "What's up?" John asked.

"I ran into a friend of mine coming out of the liquor store. I can't go in there now. He'll know something's up."

"Why?" asked John.

"Because he knows I don't drink."

John stared at Michael. "Isn't he your boyfriend from the Pizza Palace?"

"He's not my boyfriend." I could feel myself blushing. "But he'll think something's fishy if I don't walk home with him."

John gave me a grin, as if he didn't believe me. "Go on, Dani. You've done a good day's work. We'll get this store first thing Thursday. Go have some fun. Your boyfriend's cute."

"I told you, he's not my boyfriend."

John started to pull away from the curb before I could even close the door.

"What gives?" Michael said when I got back. "Wasn't that the cop from the Pizza Palace?"

"Oh, yes. . . ."

"A friend of the family?"

I closed my eyes for a second. Everything was getting so complicated. "Yes," I said. "He and my dad know each other from court. My dad knows lots of cops."

"What's making you so nervous? I'm the one who's suposed to be nervous around cops."

"It's nothing!" I knew Michael was just teasing me. But the lies seemed to be piling up between us.

ELEVEN

At lunch Thursday, as I sat with Bonnie and Raynor, I must have looked like I was brooding. "What's wrong, Dani?" asked Raynor. "You look so serious."

"It's nothing."

"Nothing," said Bonnie. "What about Michael?"

"That's definitely nothing."

"It doesn't look that way," said Bonnie. "It looked pretty serious the other night. What else could have you in such a dither?"

"Dither?" mocked Raynor.

"It's one of my mother's favorite words. It's a fine word."

"Very fine," agreed Raynor. I felt left out by their teasing.

"Anyhow," said Raynor, "lighten up, Dani. You're taking life all too seriously these days."

"Raynor is right," said Bonnie. "Come on. It's almost time for our next class. We'd better clean up."

Bonnie and Raynor stood up as one, connected by an invisible string. I still hoped things would snap back to normal between the three of us. Yet somehow I didn't believe it would ever be exactly the same again.

Michael tapped me lightly on the shoulder on the way to class and I whirled around.

"Hey, it's just me, not the vice squad."

"I'm a little jumpy," I said. "I've got a test next period."

"Well, how about celebrating when it's over? How about going for a drive after school? No booze, I promise you. It's a beautiful day. We could even go to the shore."

It sounded wonderful. But I couldn't do it. I had to meet John.

Michael saw the disappointed look on my face. "I forgot. You've got to work, don't you. Another time?" he asked.

"Love to," I said, not bothering to correct Michael about exactly what kind of work I had to do. I did have work. Undercover work.

Michael shrugged. "We'll do it another time."

"When?" I asked quickly. Then I blushed.

But Michael didn't make fun of me. "How about tomorrow night? A movie or something?"

"Great," I said.

"Okay, I'll pick you up around seven."

Michael had finally asked me out, even if I had pushed him just a little. Suddenly everything in my life seemed much better. I practically skipped down the hall to class. Bonnie saw me in the hall.

"What happened?" she asked. "You look like you're flying."

"Michael finally asked me out on a real date," I said, a little bit scared that she would make some crack about his being drunk.

"That's super," she said. I wanted to hug her, but she hugged me first.

I was still in a good mood after school when I went to the park to meet John. It was a beautiful spring day. The park was full of kids, and as I waited for John, I began to hope that he wouldn't show. It was too beautiful a day to have to go into dingy liquor stores and lie to clerks. I wanted to be free to enjoy it.

I really wasn't looking forward to having to work with John again. If I had to work, I would have preferred to work with Jessica.

It was true that I hadn't liked Jessica when we first met. But I liked the way she went after what she wanted—the Corvette, her job. She didn't take any bull from anyone. And she had warned me about John. "Take everything John Nelson says with a grain of salt," she had said. At the time I didn't know what to think, but now I wondered. Could there be something going on that I hadn't realized? Had John not been straight when he recruited me?

John's tires squealed as he drove into the park and stopped in front of me. "Sorry I'm late," he said, as I got into the car. He seemed more preoccupied than ever.

"I was beginning to think you wouldn't show up," I said.

"Think or hope?"

"Look," I said angrily."I'm not getting paid for this. If something I'm doing is bothering you, I wish you'd tell me."

"I'm sorry, Dani. I told you before. It's got nothing to do with you. It's just a departmental matter. Nothing personal. I meant to apologize for the lousy mood I was in last time."

He reached across the steering wheel and held his hand out. "Shake?"

I shook his hand. I still didn't understand what was going on, but I was glad it wasn't something I was doing.

"We'll start with the Grog and Grape," said John. "Okay?"

I wasn't sure that it was okay. I had been feeling creepy about the Grog and Grape ever since I discovered that Michael's cousin worked there. Should I tell John that my friend was related to the clerk? I didn't want him to make any cracks about "my boyfriend." Maybe Michael's cousin wouldn't be working today. I tried to put Michael out of my mind. He'd hate it if he knew what I was doing.

John seemed determined to make up for the bad mood he had been in before. He poured on the charm, but it seemed artificial. He told me that I looked good, that everyone in the police department was glad that I was volunteering to help them; but nothing he said sounded sincere. It was flattering to hear, but I just didn't believe him. I wanted to tell him that he didn't have to try so hard.

We pulled up in front of the Grog and Grape. Tequila wasn't outside again. That was a good sign.

"This store is the last one we'll be hitting," John said. "After this, it'll all be over until the DA goes before the grand jury."

"Are you glad it's almost over?" I asked.

John looked nervous. "Why do you ask?"

I shrugged. "I just feel like you've changed your mind about this program. When you came to my house you sounded much more enthusiastic. Or was that just an act for my parents?"

"Dani, I've already told you. My mood has nothing to do with you . . . you or the program. Stop reading more into my words than I mean. Off you go now.'' He winked at me as I got out of the car. "Good luck," he said.

He seemed to emphasize the word *luck*, as if he knew that I'd need it. I walked into the Grog and Grape feeling very uneasy.

TWELVE

Just my luck—Michael's cousin was behind the counter waiting on two guys. One of them was about six feet six. The other was short only by comparison, about five eleven.

I put down my knapsack, picked up a wine bottle, and studied its label. It cost $24.98. And it was only from California. I thought wines from California were supposed to be cheap.

Suddenly I heard a sharp, popping noise, like a loud champagne cork. The tall guy was holding a black gun in his hand. It looked like a toy, but Michael's cousin had turned pale. I could see a broken bottle on the shelf behind him. Dark brown liquid poured down on the floor.

"Another move and the next one will be in your face," said the tall guy. "Now open the register."

I didn't think the robbers realized I was in the store. If I could get out, I could get John from around the corner. My heart was beating so hard, I was sure somebody would hear it.

Michael's cousin was looking straight at me as I inched toward the door. Suddenly the guy with the gun whirled around, pointing the gun directly at me.

"Please, please. I won't—" I don't know what I was going to tell them that I wouldn't do.

The guy holding the gun was shaking, too. The gun wobbled in his hand, but it was pointed straight at my belly.

"Please . . . please . . ." It was the only word I could come up with.

"Over here," said the guy.

I took a step and I was shaking so much that I almost fell flat on my face.

"Move," commanded the guy.

I felt as if I were suffocating. I couldn't get air into my lungs.

"Hurry," said the shorter guy. He was wearing a black T-shirt. He grabbed me by the arm and half flung me toward the counter. I had to brace myself to keep from sprawling over it.

If only John would realize that something was wrong. I prayed for my life. I was a witness. I wondered if the guy with the gun was going to shoot me.

"Here's your money," said Michael's cousin. He flung a fistful of bills onto the counter.

The short guy shoved the money into a brown paper bag. "Let's get out of here," he said.

"Wait a minute," snapped the guy with the gun. He grabbed me by my arm. His breath was vile, and I thought I was going to throw up.

He was so strong I couldn't pull away. He dragged me effortlessly toward the door. "Please, just leave me here," I cried. I tasted tears in my mouth. "I won't tell."

He shoved me toward the door. Then I heard a voice shout, "Duck!"

I threw myself on the floor, my hands over my head, trying to make myself as small as possible. A gun went off. I kept my hands over my head. My eyes were shut tight. All I could think of was that I didn't want to die.

Then I felt a hand on my shoulder. "Are you all right?" a voice asked urgently. I didn't recognize the voice at first.

Very slowly, I lifted my head. Another gun was pointed at me, but it was Jessica who was holding it. I began to cry.

I couldn't understand why Jessica was there. How had she appeared—like magic? And where was John? Then I saw him standing by the counter talking to Michael's cousin.

Jessica helped me up. "How did you get here?" I whispered.

Jessica shook her head, warning me that I had to act as if I didn't know her. I was still undercover.

I dusted myself off. Jessica gave me an encouraging smile. "I'm all right," I said.

"You certainly have a knack for finding trouble," she whispered.

"Believe me," I said. "This didn't have anything to do with me. I was so scared I thought I was going to die."

"Hush," said Jessica. "You're all right now. You're safe."

"But I still don't understand what you're doing here," I said.

"This shop is wired with a silent alarm. I heard the call go out over the radio, and I remembered that you and John were going to come here today. I got here in record time."

"Thanks," I said.

Jessica turned to listen to something that Michael's cousin was saying. At first I couldn't catch the words. Then I heard them, and I thought I was going crazy.

Michael's cousin was pointing a finger at me. "She was with them," he was saying. "The money's in her knapsack. She's one of the robbers!"

THIRTEEN

I went numb with shock. I thought I was losing my mind.

"Look in her knapsack," Michael's cousin repeated.

"I don't understand," I said. "The guy with the gun—you saw him force me to go with him. The short guy's got the money."

"They got away," John said. "There was a car waiting for them outside." I barely heard him. I was so relieved to be alive. Now that John and Jessica were there, I was sure everything would work out.

"Please tell this guy he's wrong," I said.

"I can't tell him anything," said John furiously. "I was sitting right outside and I never realized anything was wrong."

Jessica was holding my knapsack. She had picked it up off the floor.

"I tell you, she was with them! The money's in her knapsack," insisted Michael's cousin.

Jessica put my knapsack on the counter.

"You'll see," I said. "There's no money in it. He's lying."

"Let's take a look," John said. But when he turned his eyes on me, I froze.

Michael's cousin was looking at me as if I were a lousy, creepy criminal. The fact that I was supposed

to keep my undercover work a secret wasn't important to me anymore. What was more important was
that John and Jessica would tell Michael's cousin I
couldn't possibly have been involved in the robbery.

John pulled on the drawstring of my knapsack and
reached inside. The first thing he pulled out was a
brown paper bag.

"That's not mine," I cried. It was as if Harry
Houdini himself had somehow managed to pull off
the magic trick of the century.

Jessica gave me a warning look. "What else is in
there?" she asked.

John pulled out my chemistry book and a sweat-
shirt. Then he reached back and came out with a
plastic baggie. It was full of marijuana. It wasn't
mine! I knew it wasn't there when I left school. But
who would believe me?

John flipped open my book. My name was written
on the inside cover. "Danielle Nelli?" he asked, as
if he had never heard the name before. "You have
the right to remain silent. You have the right to
counsel. You should be aware that anything you say
may be used against you. We are conducting this
search of your knapsack because we found you at the
scene of a crime with probable cause. Would you
like to call a lawyer?"

I stared at Jessica and John. Jessica wouldn't look
at me. John stared at the ground. Could he actually
believe I might have had anything to do with the
robbery?

"I want to call my dad. He's a lawyer," I said.

"You can call down at the station," said Jessica.
She turned to Michael's cousin. "You'll have to
come, too, and make a statement."

"I can't leave the store," he protested. "I'll tell

you what happened. She walked in with the two other guys.''

"I did not! They were already at the counter!"

"I advise you to keep quiet until you have a lawyer with you," said John formally.

"She pretended to be looking at some wine bottles," said Michael's cousin. "But I knew something was fishy. She's much too young to buy liquor. I would never have sold her anything."

My mouth dropped open. This wasn't just some crazy misunderstanding. I felt like an animal in a trap. He was deliberately lying about me. Until then, I thought he just might be in shock and not know what he was saying. But he wasn't in shock anymore. He was telling out-and-out lies. And Jessica and John seemed to believe him.

"The tall guy pulled a gun on me," Michael's cousin continued. "He asked for the money from the register. That's when she came up to the counter and joined them."

I remembered how it had felt with the the gun pointed at me, the stench of the robber's breath when he forced me to come forward. There was no way that Michael's cousin couldn't have known that I was innocent. He *had* to have seen that the gun was pointed at me as well as at him.

"I thought they were going to kill us both," I blurted out.

"That's when I pushed the alarm buzzer. I handed over the money. I saw them put it in her knapsack, and then they started to leave. She went first."

"Because I had a gun in my back!" I screamed. I had to fight back sobs. "Why won't you say you know me?" I pleaded with Jessica and John. "You've got to know I'm innocent! I can't be arrested, can I?"

"Just keep quiet, Danielle," John said. "You've already said too much. I'm going to take you in. I don't think we need handcuffs."

"Handcuffs?" I echoed.

"Let's go," said John gruffly. He turned to Michael's cousin. "I'm sorry. But you will have to come down to the police station to make a formal statement."

John took me by the upper arm and marched me out of the liquor store. Michael's cousin followed. John half pushed and half shoved me into the back-seat of his car.

John got behind the steering wheel and drove us to the municipal building. I stared out the window, trying hard not to cry. I tried to remember every detail, so that I could try to explain what had happened to my father. No matter which way I turned the events, they just didn't make any sense. They didn't add up.

FOURTEEN

I was put into lockup while they called my parents. I was alone in a small room, about six feet by ten. There were no windows. When I tried the door and it was locked, I had to fight down a feeling of panic. I sat down on one of the six wooden chairs in the room. That was it for furniture—just six wooden chairs. I wondered why they needed six.

I wanted to bang on the door and plead with them to let me out.

John and Jessica had abandoned me when we arrived at the police department. I wanted them to say, "This is ridiculous. Obviously you're being framed. You'd be the last person to be involved in a robbery. You were with the police." That's what I wanted someone to say. I was being framed, and my two *friends* on the police force acted as if they never even considered a setup.

Could they think that Michael's cousin was telling the truth? Maybe they even thought that I had planned the robbery from the beginning, that I had volunteered just to make fools of the police.

Could they possibly believe that? I forced myself to admit that they could. But the robbery wasn't real. It was all an elaborate charade to frame me.

But why me? I was just a sixteen-year-old kid.

Finally the door opened. My father stood there. He looked pale. But he held his arms out to me. I went flying across the room and buried my face in his shoulder. His arms went around my back, holding me tight. No matter what happened, he was there. I sobbed and sobbed until I finally ran out of tears.

My father wiped my tears away the way he used to when I was a little kid. "Be careful," he whispered. "Your face might freeze like that."

It was an old family joke. When I was little and had cried, my father had always said, "Be careful, your face might freeze."

I wished I was a little girl again. But I knew Mommy and Daddy couldn't make everything all right now. Not this nightmare.

"Okay, Dani," said my father. "Tell me exactly what happened, from the beginning."

I told my father how I was framed. He kept looking at me as if I were crazy.

"The worst part is that I'm not even sure that John believes me. Even Jessica just stared at me. It's as if they've forgotten why I was in the liquor store to begin with."

"We'll see about this," my father said angrily. He took me by the hand. He signaled the guard outside of lockup to come and get us.

"I'm taking her to see Officer Nelson and Officer Martin," said my father.

"I'm sorry, sir, but she has to remain in lockup."

"No!" said my father. He didn't shout, but the guard stiffened. "You can come with us, but she is not staying in that room alone."

Just then John, Jessica, and Michael's cousin came down the hall. They were whispering together. A strange man was following them.

73

"It's all right," said John. "You can let her out. We were just coming to get you anyway."

I felt a wave of relief. John was coming to get me. They were going to admit that it had all been a horrible mistake. Michael's cousin had explained that he had lied. He had explained how the money and the marijuana had gotten into my knapsack.

The stranger moved forward. I was blinded by a flashbulb inches from my face. I ducked my head involuntarily just as another flash went off.

"Robert Miller from the Morristown *Times*," he said. "Is this the suspect in the liquor-store robbery?"

"Yes," said Michael's cousin. "She was one of the robbers."

"How did you get here so fast?" my father snapped at the reporter.

"Picked it up on the police radio," he answered. "This story could be news. We don't get that many teenage girls robbing liquor stores."

"Get out of here," my father growled.

"Hey, we have a free press around here."

"Just leave my daughter alone," said my father.

"Don't I know you? Aren't you Ed Nelli from the legal aid office?"

"Get out of my way," said my father. He kept my hand firmly in his. "John," he shouted, "I want to talk to you—privately."

Both John and Jessica came over. Neither of them seemed to want to look my father in the eye. "I don't think we should speak in private now," said John. "We all need time to sort this thing out. We've spoken to the DA," said John. "Dani can go without bail. We'll release her to you."

"Release her," snapped my father. "I want you to drop all charges. This is outrageous."

74

"I'm sorry," said John. "I'd like to. But we can't. There is too much evidence against her."

"She was obviously framed."

"But who would want to frame her? Why? It doesn't make sense."

My father made an effort to control himself. "You came to Dani. *You* asked her to volunteer. You wanted to use her as an undercover agent to catch liquor stores selling to minors. We're talking about a good student, a girl who has never been in trouble with the police in her life. Now you're accusing her of being mixed up with two hoods she's never even seen before."

"Please, Mr. Nelli," John said. "Try to look at it from our point of view. We have egg on our face. As far as we know, the liquor-store clerk had no reason to lie. We found the money in Dani's knapsack, along with almost an ounce of marijuana. We're the ones who feel set up. The entire program is ruined. Can you imagine our bringing Dani before a grand jury to testify? We'd be laughed out of court."

"But . . . but . . ." sputtered my father. "She's innocent!"

"That's where you and I differ," said John. "I'm not so sure."

I left the police station with my father. He was responsible for making sure that I showed up for my arraignment. *Arraignment*. I had never understood what the word meant. Now I knew. It meant that the police thought they had enough evidence against me to bring me to trial. Proving myself innocent might not be so easy after all.

FIFTEEN

The next day my picture was in the newspaper. TEEN SUSPECT IN LIQUOR STORE HEIST. It gave my name and everything. It said that I had claimed to be an undercover agent for the police. "The police had no comment."

I thought I was going to die.

My father grunted when he showed it to me at breakfast. "It's my fault," he said. "I forgot that stupid reporter was there when I was arguing with John. That's how he got the stuff about your being an undercover agent."

The only thing that had gotten me through the previous night was that my mom and dad believed me. At least *they* trusted me. No talk about my judgment or lack of it. They were one hundred percent behind me. It didn't seem like anybody else was. And now the whole world was going to know about it.

Mom threw down the paper with disgust. "How can they print this pack of lies? They make Dani sound tried and convicted."

"They say alleged, Mom." I picked up the paper and read it again. "I hate John and Jessica. How could they make no comment?"

Mom leaned across the table and gave my arm a

squeeze. "We'll make them eat their words, especially the 'no comment.' "

"That's not going to do me any good if I wind up in jail," I said. "Or reform school."

"You're not going to jail!" my father said. "Believe me, you're not spending one second in jail."

"Innocent people have been sent to jail before," I said. "You've said that yourself. How can you be sure I won't be one of them?"

"Dani, I'm sure," said my father.

I didn't say anything more. I knew my dad wanted me to believe that he could save me. But he hadn't been there. He didn't realize yet just how much evidence they had against me.

Just then the phone rang. We all looked at each other. "I meant to take it off the hook," my mother said.

"You might as well answer it," said my father. "You'll have to talk to our friends today, anyhow."

Mom went to the phone. "Dani, it's Bonnie. She read the paper. Do you want to talk to her?"

I nodded. I was scared. Would she believe what she had read?

"Dani, are you okay? What happened?" Bonnie's words tumbled out, full of concern. It didn't matter what the words were. I just felt good hearing her voice. I knew she was with me.

"Oh, Bonnie, it was awful, a nightmare. It was the creepiest thing in the world."

"Look, Raynor and I want to come over. He's read the paper, too, and he's over here. He said he bets you were set up. Can we pick you up on the way to school? Are you going? Raynor thought you might stay home."

"I haven't even thought about it."

"I think you should go," said Bonnie. "I'll punch out the first kid who makes a crack."

I couldn't imagine Bonnie punching anyone out.

"Look, can you come over for a few minutes, anyhow? I just need to see you. I'll decide about school. I'll have to talk to my parents about it."

I hung up. I told my parents that I wanted to go to school, even with all the publicity.

"Dani, are you sure?" my mom asked. "I think maybe you should just take it easy today."

"No . . . I want to go. It'll be better than staying home and imagining that everyone is talking about me. And Bonnie's phone call made me feel better."

"You've got a lot of courage," said my dad.

I couldn't tell him the truth. I would feel helpless staying home, and I would have to watch him and Mom feeling helpless.

The phone rang again. I knew it would be ringing off the hook all day. My grandparents, my aunts and uncles, friends of the family . . . no, I didn't want to stay home.

I went to the front window to look out for Bonnie and Raynor. A truck had driven up with the Channel 7 emblem on its side.

A television crew got out of the truck and began setting up cameras on our lawn. I recognized Kristie Kelly, the Channel 7 reporter. She rang our doorbell.

"What should we do?" I asked Mom.

"I'm going to tell them to get off our lawn. You stay away from the front door. You don't need any more publicity."

Just then Raynor and Bonnie turned up, and Kristie Kelly pounced on them. I could see her shove her microphone in front of Bonnie. Bonnie stopped. She looked flustered, but she straightened her hair. So did Raynor.

As soon as my mother opened the door, the TV crew abandoned Bonnie and Raynor and dashed for our front steps.

"Mrs. Nelli," shouted Kristie Kelly. "May we interview your daughter?"

Mom shoved Bonnie and Raynor inside. "My daughter is innocent. We have no other comment."

She slammed the door shut. Raynor saw me standing behind the door. His first move was to hug me. I was touched. It was so unlike Raynor. I would have expected him to greet me with some sarcastic crack, but all he did was hug me. Bonnie hugged me, too. I needed those hugs.

I had tears in my eyes when we separated.

"So that's what it's like to be a celebrity," said Raynor. "I knew you were a ham, but I think you went too far this time." The joke was feeble, but it was the first time in a long time that I had laughed.

"Anything for fame," I said.

"I knew it all the time," said Raynor. "You pulled off a daring liquor-store robbery just so you could get your picture in the paper. Well, it makes as much sense as that story in the newspaper."

"So tell us what really happened," said Bonnie.

Quickly I told them everything that had happened— from my decision to work undercover with the police to how Michael's cousin had lied. "So you see, the scary part is that it's almost like the newspaper story," I said. "All the evidence points to me."

Raynor looked more and more furious. "The lying creep," he said. "We should go break his kneecaps."

"That'll do Dani a lot of good," said Bonnie.

"Well, we've got to do something," said Raynor.

"You kids had better stay out of it," my mother interrupted. "Dani's father is going to handle her defense."

But a plan was beginning to take shape in my head. I would need Bonnie and Raynor. I couldn't tell my parents about it, at least not yet.

"We've got a problem, Mom," I said. "How are we going to get out of here to go to school? It looks like a movie set out there. We're under siege. Do you think they'll follow us to school?"

Mom pulled aside the living-room curtain. Dad was on the phone to his office. I had never seen Mom look so awful. She looked much older than she had ever looked before. I couldn't stand to see her looking so upset. "I'll drive you to school," she said. "I don't want you to run that gauntlet out there. We can leave through the garage, and we'll lock the doors. We're not going to be prisoners in our own home." The more Mom talked, the better she looked. She lost that hopeless look in her eyes.

Dad got off the phone. "My office has offered to do anything to help. We're going to get some investigators on that liquor clerk. . . ." The phone rang again. "I should have left it off the hook," my father moaned.

We felt like sneak thieves trying to get out of our own house. Raynor sat up front next to Mom. I sat in the backseat with my head in Bonnie's lap.

Mom opened the garage door and shot down the driveway. A couple of TV reporters rushed after us. When we were a couple of blocks away, Bonnie told me that I could come up for air. No one was following us.

Mom drove around the school once before she let us out. She wanted to make sure that no reporters had staked out the school. The coast looked clear. As we got out of the car, Mom turned to give me a hug. She held on tight, as if she thought she'd never see me again.

"I'll be okay, Mom, honest," I said.

"I know," she said.

I hugged her again. I didn't tell her that I wasn't at all sure I was going to be okay. I was scared to go to school, scared of what my friends might say. Most of all, I was scared about seeing Michael again. What would he think, now that he knew I had been working with the police? And what would he think when he realized his own cousin had accused me of armed robbery?

SIXTEEN

I walked up the steps to school between Bonnie and Raynor, my bodyguards. I would never have survived that day without them.

"I feel like I'm a stool pigeon or something," I whispered bitterly to Raynor, as out of the corner of my eye I saw someone point to me.

"Everyone's just curious," said Raynor. "They don't mean to be nasty."

Later I realized that Raynor was right. It wasn't all bad. Kids came up to me to tell me they didn't believe the story in the newspaper. Mr. Oppenheimer, my science teacher, told me he would be glad to testify as a character witness. He was so kind that he made me blush, and he wasn't the only teacher to offer support.

But still it was a nightmare. One kid hissed "jail-bait" as I walked down the hall. Bonnie whirled around. "What did you say?" she glared at him. He was a kid none of us knew. He stared down at the ground. "Nothing," he muttered, and then he scurried down the hall, like a rat.

Bonnie watched him go. She gave me a worried glance. "See," she said, trying to be cheery. "You didn't have to worry. I didn't hit him."

"Thanks," I said. "For everything. I mean it."

She shrugged. "We're friends, remember?"

I smiled. "Yes," I said, "I remember."

The day was exhausting. I hadn't realized how tired I was. I certainly didn't learn anything in any of my classes, and I don't think anyone else did much learning, either. By two o'clock, I could barely hold my head up. I walked into advanced history, grateful that it was the last class of the day, but I was also dreading it because I knew I'd have to see Michael. I hadn't seen him all day, so I figured he was purposely avoiding me.

Michael was sitting in the back of the room. When he saw me, he looked out the window. I held my head up and sat down near the front.

Everything had started with Michael—the night that we hit the dog. It was *his* cousin who had framed me. And now he wouldn't even look me in the eye.

I wanted to put my head down on the desk and just collapse. I could have gotten excused from class, but getting through the whole day had become a matter of pride to me, probably stupid pride.

Finally the class was over. I could see Bonnie and Raynor waiting for me outside. I gathered my books and headed for the door. Michael stopped me. "Wait, Dani," he said. "Please, I have to talk to you alone."

Raynor stepped in front of me before I could answer. "Look, Michael," he said. "We know it was your cousin who accused Dani. Where does that leave you?"

Michael looked angry. "What kind of idiot do you take me for? I know Dani'd be the last person in the world to have dope in her knapsack. I know she doesn't go around holding up liquor stores. I know my cousin must be lying. I can't believe this whole thing. Dani, an undercover agent! Come on, that reporter must have been smoking that stuff they found in her knapsack.''

"It's true. I was an undercover agent. It's the only true part. I was working with the police. They were trying to crack down on liquor stores that sold to minors.''

Michael looked from Raynor to me. Everyone in the hall was staring at us.

"Michael," I said, "I'm sorry, but we can't talk about this now. I don't want to come between you and your cousin. We're on opposite sides now.''

"No! Don't do this to me, Dani. I'll pick what side I'm on. I know things about my cousin that might help. You can't just shut me out.'' Michael calmed down. He looked me in the eye. "Besides," he said, "we have a date tonight, remember?''

I had completely forgotten about it. It felt like we had made that date a lifetime ago.

"Let me help," Michael said.

"Let him help," echoed Bonnie. She sounded so sincere that Michael, Raynor, and I all started to laugh.

Raynor stopped laughing. "Dani, you need all the help you can get.''

"Okay," I said. "Michael, you are now officially part of the Dani Defense Committee. Only now, we've got to come up with a defense.''

"We will," said Michael. "I'm good at chess. I should be good at strategy.''

"This isn't a game.''

"I know it's real," said Michael. "You don't have to remind me.''

"It was real, all right," I said. "I remember the gun in the guy's hand. It was very real. Real enough to go off and break a liquor bottle.''

"But nobody got hurt," said Michael.

"I thought I was going to get killed."

Michael looked thoughtful. "Still, I'm curious. I wonder how the robber managed to hit a bottle on a shelf, but missed the cops."

"We were lucky," I said.

"I wonder," Michael mused.

SEVENTEEN

We didn't want to go back to my house where there might still be reporters, so we went to the park. We found a place to sit that was just a little bit hidden away. I put my head in my arms. I literally couldn't stand up. Michael sat beside me and massaged my shoulders and my neck. I hadn't realized how tense I must have been. The tendons between my neck and shoulder were so tight I could hear the muscles crackle as Michael tried to loosen me up.

"It's like you've got a metal rod in your shoulders," he said, as his fingers tenderly dug into my sore muscles. "Does that feel okay?" he asked.

"It feels wonderful," I said gratefully. I lifted my head a couple of inches off the grass.

Raynor gave me a knowing grin. "You don't look like you're suffering."

"Michael, do you think you can come and visit me in jail?" I asked.

"You're not going to jail," said Bonnie.

"Thanks, but you're too young to be on the jury."

"As soon as it comes out what you were doing for the police, they're going to have to drop the charges."

"That's what I thought, and Dad thought, but we were wrong. I've got no protection. In fact, the police seem to think that I planned the robbery because I was counting on the fact that I could get off.''

Michael stopped massaging my neck. "Why did you do it? I mean, work for the police, not knock over a liquor store.''

I thought about it. Bonnie and Raynor were staring at me, too, waiting for me to give some kind of answer. "It's not easy to explain," I said.

"Hey, you don't need to explain anything," said Raynor.

"Thanks," I said. "But it's a fair question and not so simple. The police wanted me. And they asked me at a time when no one else was falling over me. I sort of liked having a secret life. It was glamorous and for a good cause. And you know my parents' reputations for getting involved with causes. It was as if there was a yardstick I had to live up to, and working with the police gave me a step up. And then it was fun to try to go into liquor stores and fool them. I know that doesn't sound right, but it was. I don't know . . . I'm not making any sense, am I?''

"A little," said Raynor. "It's weird that you would have kept something like this a secret from us. We always used to tell each other everything.''

"Dani," said Bonnie, "we haven't been real straight with you, either.''

"More secrets?''

"Not anything like yours," said Bonnie. "It's just that the night of the party, well, you and Michael weren't the only two who—''

"Went out and hit a dog?" Michael teased. "I'm sorry," he said. "But everyone can see that you two have become more than just friends.''

"You mean you two started to get something going

romantically . . . after all these years of being just friends?'' I said in a shocked voice.

Raynor nodded.

"It was obvious," said Michael.

"Not to me," I said. "I was too preoccupied with myself. I guess I was pretty dumb."

"We were scared to tell you," said Raynor. "It had been the three of us for so long, we thought you might be mad."

I shook my head. "No . . . I just feel silly that you felt you couldn't tell me."

"Well," said Michael, "now that we've settled the important stuff, like who's going with whom, let's get back to Dani's problem. I'd like a chance to go out with Dani without having to worry about visiting her in jail."

"If only I hadn't gone into the Grog and Grape the exact moment of the robbery. I have lousy luck."

"Quite a coincidence," said Michael. "So that's what you were doing at the Grog and Grape the day I saw you. I knew you didn't like drinking. I didn't realize it was a crusade."

"It wasn't," I said. "It wasn't a crusade. The police asked me to help, and I agreed."

"Stop being so defensive," said Michael. "Who said there was anything wrong with being a crusader? Maybe you were doing the right thing."

"Even though it was your cousin!" I shouted.

"Look," said Bonnie, "this isn't getting us anywhere. I thought we were going to brainstorm a way to help Dani."

"I think we should just forget it," I said. "I'd better go home. There's nothing we can do, anyhow. My dad's a good lawyer. He'll think of something." I tried to sound brave, but I didn't feel very optimistic. "There's nothing you can do, nothing I can do. I set out to trap people who were breaking the law, and I wound up in a trap made out of steel."

"That's it," said Michael. "The police used Dani as bait. Oh, yes, Dani, that's what you were . . . jail-bait."

"Jailbait. That's what a kid in school called me, and Bonnie almost punched him out."

"Don't punch me out, just hear me out," Michael said. "Now, who benefits if the bait herself gets put in jail? Who benefits? *Qui bono?* That's the oldest legal principal."

"We all know you took Latin," said Raynor.

"I'm not showing off," objected Michael. "Think about who gains from throwing Dani in jail."

"Well, your cousin gains," I said. "He sold me liquor before, and he probably would have again. All the crooked liquor store owners gain. Even if I don't end up in jail, the program's ruined. No one is going to believe my testimony."

"But how did my cousin know you were working with the police?" asked Michael. "That's the real question. I don't think you just happened to go into the liquor store at the wrong moment. It wasn't any accident. That robbery was planned to happen only when you were there. I think it was phony from the beginning. It sounds like it came straight off the TV screen.

"I know my cousin," continued Michael. "He's not a bad guy, but he's not particularly swift. When we were kids, our nickname for him was Brains 'cause he didn't have many. There's no way he could have pulled this off."

"Forget about how smart he is," said Bonnie. "Somebody had to tip him off. Who else knew about the program? You kept it a secret from us. Besides the police and your parents, who knew about it?"

"No one," I said. "The only ones who knew exactly what stores we were going to each day were John and Jessica. But John recruited me. They were one hundred percent behind the program."

"Well, it had to be someone," said Michael. "Somebody set you up, and it wasn't just my cousin."

"Look, kids," said Bonnie. "We still need a brilliant, inspirational plan that will solve everything."

"It means a lot to me that you tried to help," I said. I felt exhausted again. All I wanted to do was to go home and sleep.

"Dani, will you stop trying out for sainthood," snapped Raynor. "I can't take this resigned act. You sound like you're about to go off to the electric chair."

"Yes, Saint Dani of the Undercover. I'm the perfect candidate." I laughed, and then I started to cry. "I'm sorry," I gasped, trying to make myself stop. "I cried all last night. I thought I was done."

Raynor put his arm around me. "You can cry all you want to."

"Like that old song," I sniffed. "It's my party and I'll cry if I want to."

Bonnie broke in harmonizing. "You would cry, too . . . if it happened to you."

"Unless you prefer to cry about it, I've got an idea," Michael said. "My cousin doesn't know that I'm a friend of Dani's. Maybe he'll talk to me, and maybe Dani should come along. If he sees you with me, he may be willing to tell the truth."

"Do you really think he'll talk to me?" I asked. "I think when he sees me he'll run."

"He'll want to know what's going on," said Raynor. "Surprise is the only weapon we've got."

"Right now?" I asked. I was hoping Michael meant that we should try it tomorrow.

"Yeah. If we wait, he'll just get more and more sure of himself. He might even find out that I know you. I have to pick up Tequila . . ." Michael paused. He turned to Bonnie and Raynor. "That's the name of my dog. I don't mean pick up a bottle."

"We know," said Bonnie.

"Anyway, Dani, why don't you come home with me and we'll go from there." He turned to Bonnie and Raynor. "Too many people will scare him off. I think just Dani and I should go."

I didn't feel ready. To tell the truth, I was more than a little scared.

"Don't worry," said Michael, "but even if today's a washout, I think we should make plans to meet again tomorrow."

"Right," said Bonnie. "The Dani Nelli Defense Committee. Let's hope it's the shortest-lived club in school history."

Michael held his hand out to me. "Let's go, tiger," he said.

"Tiger? I feel like a pussycat that someone tried to drown."

"No," said Michael. "You've been knocked down, but you're not out—not by a long shot."

EIGHTEEN

Tequila seemed happy to see us. Overjoyed would be more like it. He jumped up and licked Michael's face.

"Sorry I'm late, boy. I know, you've got to go out." Michael got the dog's leash and we went out. Tequila's coat shone in the sunlight.

"He really looks healthy," I said. "You're taking good care of him."

"Surprised?"

"No. Don't be so defensive. I wasn't trying to criticize you."

Michael laughed. "You're the one who's usually on the defensive."

"I'm not. I'm just in that position now. But it's not normal for me. I'm sorry you think that."

"I don't. I don't know why I said that. You make me think about my life. Maybe it was just that accident. It scared me."

"It scared me, too."

"That night I wandered over to your house and we kissed. . . . I could tell you pulled away when you smelled liquor on my breath. I decided to try to stop drinking altogether."

"Have you stopped?"

"I've been trying. Look, it's not as if I have a

magic wand I can wave. Whoopee—I've stopped drinking. It's not like that.''

"I know," I said. "Nothing is black and white, is it? But you have guts, Michael. I think it takes guts to decide to change.'' I thought a moment. "I'm not sure that I have that kind of guts. Maybe wanting to go undercover was my way of taking a shortcut.''

"Don't make me into some kind of hero,'' said Michael. "You've got plenty of guts. You're just not perfect. But I don't know who told you you had to be.''

I took Michael's hand. "Okay, no hero. . . . But I can like you, can't I?'' I asked.

"Well, maybe I'll give you permission.'' He didn't try to pull his hand away.

We walked down the street holding hands. I liked the feel of his hand in mine. "It's weird isn't it?'' I said.

"What's weird?''

I shrugged my shoulders. "Life.''

"Yeah, well, you know what Hunter Thompson says: 'When the going gets weird, the weird turn pro.' Life is weird all right, but it doesn't have to be this weird.''

We walked awhile without saying anything. I just liked Michael—a lot. If wondered if he knew how much.

"Still feeling scared?'' Michael asked.

"Nope,'' I said. "That's not what I was thinking.''

"You want me to guess?''

"You can try.''

"You're thinking about what kind of food you'll get in jail. Do you want me to bring you Pizza Palace Specials?''

"No . . . that would be the worst—jail and Pizza

Palace food. I hate Pizza Palace Specials. I get so sick of the smell of pizza. If you bring me that in jail, I'll kill you.''

"All right, you're not thinking about pizza. You must be thinking about me.''

"Come on, Michael. Do you want me to tell you I've got a crush on you?'' I tried to sound like I was just teasing.

Michael put his hand on my chin and lifted it. "Come on, Dani . . . we've been through too much. A crush sounds so *cute* . . . that's not what you meant.''

I swallowed hard. Michael was right. I was trying to make it all sound light and cute. "No . . . it's more than a crush.''

"For me, too,'' said Michael. He kissed me, hard on the lips. Tequila sat down and watched us.

Finally Michael let me go. He smiled at me. "Some romance,'' he said. "Car crashes, teenage undercover agents, jail. Promise me, Dani, when everything gets straightened out, let's just go out on a normal date.''

"It's a promise,'' I said, trying to smile. We were getting closer to Michael's cousin's house. I dreaded meeting him.

"Do you think he's home?'' I asked.

"If he's not, we'll just have to go to the liquor store.''

"Oh, no,'' I said. "I came here with you. But I'm not going back there.''

Michael squeezed my hand. "Okay, I won't force you. We'll cross that bridge when we come to it. Stand over by the side. He might not open the door if he sees you.''

"Terrific,'' I said. "And you think he's gonna talk to me.''

Michael rang the doorbell. We could hear it echo inside the house, but nobody came. "Nobody's home," I said quickly.

Michael jabbed his finger on the doorbell again, letting it ring several times. We heard someone scrape aside the peephole.

"Who's there?" a voice asked.

"It's me, Michael."

Slowly the door opened. Tequila rushed forward, wagging his tail. Michael's cousin bent down to pet him, and that's when he saw me.

He looked like a quarterback who'd just been tackled from his blind side. "What's she doing here?" he demanded.

Michael shut the door behind us. His cousin glared at him. "She's a friend of mine, Steve," said Michael. "We've got to talk to you."

"You've got no right," Steve sputtered.

"Relax." Michael put his arm around Steve's shoulder. Even though Steve must have been four or five years older than Michael, he was shorter and seemed like the younger one. "Nobody's going to know you talked to us."

"Is she really a friend of yours?" he asked Michael, in a voice barely above a whisper. Except for that first moment, he hadn't dared look at me again.

"She's a good friend," Michael said. He still had his arm around Steve's shoulder. "Can we go into the kitchen? Tequila could use some water. I could, too."

Steve gave me a sidelong look. "Her, too?"

"She doesn't bite," said Michael. "Did you know she was the one who saved Tequila's life? Come on, I'll tell you about it while you give Tequila some water."

We went into the kitchen. The kitchen was full of gadgets, but nothing looked used. It all looked as if it had just been unwrapped.

While Steve gave Tequila a bowl of water, Michael and I sat down at the kitchen table. Michael gave my shoulder a little squeeze as he pulled out a chair for me, like an old-fashioned gentleman.

Steve sat down on a stool, far away from us. "You shouldn't have brought her here," he said.

"I need your help," said Michael. His voice sounded calm and confiding, as if he wasn't mad at Steve at all.

"I can't help you," said Steve. He wouldn't look at me.

"You're in a bind," said Michael.

Steve looked startled. "She's in a bind, not me."

Michael shook his head. "Did you know they can throw you in jail for perjury? That's when you lie under oath. No jury will convict her, but you'll be in trouble."

Steve's eyes widened. I could just bet that all his life Steve had been hearing how smart Michael was.

"Steve," said Michael. "She's an *A* student. She was working with the police. She comes from a good family. Do you think the jury's going to take your word over hers? Somebody's setting you up as a fall guy."

"You're crazy," said Steve. "I can't go to jail. I didn't do anything."

"You lied. You'll have to lie again in court. Come on, Steve, use your noggin. You're not as dumb as they seem to think."

Steve kept staring at Michael, looking more and more frightened. "That's not true. I'm not dumb."

"I know that. But *they* think you are. Come on,

Steve, look at her." Michael pointed to me. "She doesn't look like the kind of girl a jury would send to jail."

I held my breath. I was pretty sure that my innocent looks weren't going to be of any use if I really did have to go before a jury.

"I was told I wouldn't get in trouble."

"Whoever told you that lied," said Michael.

"But I was going to be in trouble, anyhow. You don't know how much."

"The person who told you to lie is the one in trouble," said Michael.

Steve laughed. "You must be kidding. You don't know anything."

"In big trouble," said Michael.

"A cop!" exclaimed Steve. "How is a cop going to be in trouble?"

I gasped.

Steve finally looked at me. "You didn't know, did you?"

"Which cop?" Michael asked. "Who set Dani up?"

But now Steve looked truly terrified. "I'm not going to tell you anything more. You just came here to get me in trouble."

"I didn't," protested Michael. "I came to help you."

"Get out of here," shouted Steve. "And take her with you. *Get out!*"

Michael shot a glance at me. "We'd better go," he said. "At least now we know where to look."

I stood up. A cop had set me up. Of course. Who else knew about the program? But which cop, and why? Jessica? I hadn't trusted her in the beginning, but I had come to like her. John? He had recruited me, but he had acted so strange and distant toward the end. Could John have set me up?

All I knew was that somebody had framed me. And that this somebody was a cop.

NINETEEN

I had no dreams that night. I slept deeply, as if my body and mind knew that I needed a vacation. I woke up to see the sunlight peeking through my curtains. I got out of bed and pulled the curtains aside. The day looked so beautiful, I almost cried. It seemed unfair. My life was still such a mess.

Then I told myself to can the self-pity. I remembered the feel of Michael's lips when he had kissed me good night. He had made me promise not to worry, at least until he got here Saturday morning.

I caught a glimpse of myself in the mirror over my bureau. I was shocked. The girl in the mirror was pretty. She looked lively and interesting—the kind of girl I would like. Normally, I hate the way I look in a mirror, but just then I liked my looks. In fact, I looked prettier than I expected.

Downstairs I could hear my parents whispering in the kitchen. Mom had dark circles under her eyes. I felt guilty for sleeping so well. Mom gave me a tired smile. "Well," she said. "We were a one-day wonder. The ladies and gentlemen of the press have gone off to bother someone else."

"Bonnie, Raynor, and Michael are coming over this morning. My defense committee."

Dad smiled. "Well, you need all the moral support

you can get." I caught the word "moral." I knew Dad really wanted to handle my defense alone. Last night when Michael and I had told him about our confrontation with Michael's cousin, he hadn't wanted to pursue it. "This isn't a mystery we have to solve," he said. "I just want the police to drop the charges. It's their job to figure out why all this happened. You kids don't have to wrap up all the loose ends for them. I don't want you trying to solve this on your own. I'm handling your defense."

"But, Dad, it's my life."

"I'm not denying that, Dani. I'm just saying that right now it's out of your hands."

I didn't want to fight with my father, not now. But I disagreed with him. It *was* a mystery to be solved. I needed to know who had framed me. Even if Dad got the police to drop the charges, I wouldn't be satisfied. I didn't want to go through the rest of my life as the kid who got off on a technicality.

Michael arrived first, with Tequila, of course. Bonnie and Raynor came a little later. We all sat around the kitchen table.

"So it was a cop," said Raynor. "I figured it had to be someone connected with the department."

"Not just any cop," I said. "I'm sure it had to be either John or Jessica. They were the only ones who knew exactly where I'd be. But which of them was it?"

"Let's set a trap for them," said Michael. "The final trap."

We all stared at him. "I'm not kidding," Michael said. "I told you I was good at chess. This whole thing has been like a Chinese puzzle box of traps. The police wanted to trap liquor-store owners that were breaking the law. They sent in Dani. Trap One.

Someone wanted to ruin the entrapment program. He or she discredited Dani's testimony with one move. It would have been easy for a cop to find two guys to stage that robbery. No wonder they got away. No one was trying to catch them. That's Trap Two. Now we go on the offensive with Trap Three.''

"What do you mean Trap Three?"

"The Dani Trap" said Michael. "I've fallen into it.

Raynor groaned. "Can we cut the romantic claptrap, lover boy?"

"Sorry," said Michael. "That just slipped out."

"So what's the Dani Trap? Sounds like a roach motel."

"Wrong," said Michael. "It's the perfect trap. The police don't know that Steve is my cousin. You call John and Jessica separately and tell them that Steve called you. He told you he has a guilty conscience. He wants to talk, but he warned you not to tell the police, particularly them. You say that that didn't make sense to you. Tell them that you've arranged to meet Steve at the park this afternoon at two.''

"Great," said Raynor sarcastically. "So the police will go see Steve and he'll tell them it was all a lie."

"You don't have to worry about Steve," said Michael. "He was too nervous to stick around. He called this morning to say he's driving down to the shore. No one will be able to reach him. We go to the park and wait. Whoever set Dani up will do anything to make sure that she and Steve don't meet. But we'll be ready. I brought over my tape recorder. We'll record everything."

"I don't know," said Raynor. "Won't Dani be in danger?"

"With all three of us there? We can hide behind the statue of Tom Paine. We'll have a signal. The code word will be Tequila."

"Do you think this will really work?"

"What do you have to lose?" Michael said.

"If I were you," said Raynor, "I'd want to catch the creep who framed me. This is your chance. Michael's right. You don't have anything to lose."

Michal and Raynor were right. I couldn't just leave my defense to my father. I wasn't a kid anymore. I made the phone calls. I had nothing to lose.

TWENTY

We went to the park early. There were some kids playing Frisbee in front of the Tom Paine statue. Michael got rid of them by letting Tequila off his leash. Tequila turned out to be a natural Frisbee chaser, jumping high in the air to try and catch the Frisbee on the fly. The kids soon got tired of having their Frisbee stolen by a four-legged player, so they moved on.

Then Raynor climbed a tree near the statue so he would be able to keep me in sight constantly.

I'm sure that real undercover cops do not fall out of trees. Raynor did, twice. But once he got the hang of it, I have to admit he was hard to see, and I was glad to have him there. Bonnie and Michael hid behind the statue. Michael kept Tequila on a tight leash.

We waited. I looked at my watch. 1:53. If Michael was right, someone was going to try to interrupt my meeting. He or she was cutting it awfully close.

Then I saw it. A white Corvette.

The car stopped in front of the statue. Jessica got out. She was in uniform. I could see her gun in the holster on her hip.

"Dani . . . I'm glad I got to you in time. We pulled Steve in. He's made a full confession." She opened the door to the passenger side. "Get in," she said.

I felt my heart pounding. She sounded so convincing, but if Michael was telling the truth, Steve was miles away.

"No," I said. "I don't believe you. You set me up."

"What are you talking about?"

My mouth was dry. "You didn't just pull Steve in. I lied about him calling me. I trapped you, just like you trapped me. Why did you do it?"

"Get in, Dani. We have to talk."

I shook my head and backed away. "We can talk out here," I said. The tape recorder was in my knapsack. Michael had tested it. "You wanted to discredit the program. Isn't that so?"

Jessica glanced around the park. She looked up at the tree, but missed Raynor. The park looked very deserted.

"We'll talk about all this in the car," said Jessica. She put her hand on her hip. Why hadn't I remembered that she would have a gun? "Don't be stupid, Dani," she warned me. "Get in and you won't be hurt."

"Tequila," I shouted at the top of my lungs.

Jessica grabbed for me, and I heard a voice shout, "Dani, get down!"

I threw myself on the ground.

"Hold it, Jessica. Don't even think about it." It wasn't Michael's voice. John had appeared from nowhere. His gun was drawn and it was pointed at Jessica. Two other officers were with him.

"Get up, Dani," said John. "It's all over."

Michael helped me up. Tequila tried to lick my face.

"Where did you come from?" I asked.

John kept his eyes on Jessica. "You didn't think we'd ignore your phone call, did you?" he asked. "As soon as you made it, we staked out the park. You see, I suspected Jessica was on the take. But we needed proof. That robbery was as phony as a three-dollar bill. I'm sorry you had to suffer, but we couldn't let out that we were investigating Jessica—not yet. She's been forcing all the liquor stores in the area to pay her off for looking the other way when they sold to minors. She had to think of some way to sabotage the program."

Jessica lowered her head. John turned to the two other officers. "You take her in. I don't want to be in the same car with her."

One of the officers put handcuffs on Jessica. She didn't say a word as she got into the backseat of the police cruiser. I remembered my own ride in that backseat. I didn't envy her.

John watched them drive away. Raynor climbed down from his tree. He slipped off the last branch.

"I guess I'm a little late for the rescue," he said, as he dusted himself off.

"When I got your phone call, Dani," John said, "I realized you thought that I might have set you up."

"I knew it had to be you or Jessica. My friends helped me with the final trap."

I introduced Bonnie, Raynor, and Michael to John. Michael explained that Steve was his cousin. "We'll have to question him," John said. "But if he'll testify against Jessica, I'm sure we can work something out."

"I'll talk to him," said Michael.

John took my hand. "You'll have to testify, too,

Dani. I'll talk to your parents. But we'll see that the charges are dropped, and I'm sure the Morristown *Times* will print the whole story."

"I'd better go see my parents right now." I said. "Dad's working on a way to get me off."

"You won't need a technicality," said John. "Come on. If you'd like, I'll drive you home now."

I shook my head. "Thanks, but I think I'd rather go with my Defense Committee."

John smiled. "I understand. You kids showed a lot of guts," he said. "I hope this hasn't totally turned you off police work. You know, a cop like Jessica is the odd one."

"I know."

"It's not the worst job in the world," said John. "Not by a long shot."

"Okay," I said. "I'll remember that."

"See that you do," said John. "I wouldn't mind seeing any of you on the force someday."

All that seemed very far away. I just wanted to get back to being a normal kid in high school.

John got into his car and drove away.

"Let's go," I said. "I can't wait to tell my parents I'm in the clear."

Bonnie grinned. "Hey, I've got an idea," she said. She turned to Michael. "Why don't we have a party tonight to celebrate? This time, you get a formal invitation."

Michael smiled back. "Okay," he said. "Only one thing . . ."

"What's that?" asked Raynor.

"No booze," said Michael.

"I'll drink to that," I said.